TALL, DARK 'N' TEXAN

Texas Billionaire Brothers
Book One

H.C. BROWN

I0600895

LUMINOSITY
PUBLISHING

LUMINOSITY PUBLISHING LLP

TALL, DARK 'N' TEXAN
Texas Billionaire Brothers – Book One
Copyright © November 2017 H.C. BROWN

Paperback ISBN: 978-0-9956898-9-3

Cover Art by Poppy Designs

DEDICATION

I know there are people who believe love at first sight is a myth — trust me, it's true and when it happens it lasts forever.

For my own one true love. Thanks for the many years and laughter we've spent together.

The thrilling adventure of a girl, a hurricane, and a sexy Texas cowboy

CHAPTER ONE

"I'm here at last." Susan Blake squeezed her toes into the sand and stared out across the sparkling ocean. Her attention caught by a single surfer sliding down an impressive swell. *Hmm, those waves didn't look quite so big in the brochure.*

The local news channel had given ominous warnings of a hurricane approaching the area, but apart from a line of dark clouds on the horizon, the sun shone in an expanse of blue sky. The danger appeared to be miles away and ignoring the little voice inside her head screaming, "Danger" she stepped into the foaming water. Swimming in the rough sea would be fine if she kept to the shore break. She refused to allow anything to spoil her day and splashed into the surf. *What could possibly go wrong?*

Chilled water hit hot flesh, and she gasped catching her breath. Undeterred she waded in waist deep, jumping the waves crashing around her. The next surge ripped her off her feet and exhilaration turned to dread in a millisecond. She fought the rip, but Neptune's arms reached out to seize her. Ferocious waves dragged her out to sea crashing over her and filling her mouth with salty brine. Eyes stinging and thrashing like a woman possessed, she bobbed up between waves choking and stared around to get her bearings. *Oh, shit!* Endless rolling ocean met her gaze and then as the swell lifted her, she caught sight of the beach for a split second before a wall of water hid the coastline from view.

Terrified, she caught the next wave but rather than taking her toward the beach, it carried her out to sea. Fighting against the swell was useless. With each stroke forward, the ocean dragged her deeper into its inky depths. Desperate to keep her head above water, she kicked hard and aimed for the shore, but the strong undercurrent swirled around her dragging her down like quicksand.

In a tremendous roar, another wall of water crashed over her. Helpless against the massive strength dragging her into a swirling mass of choking oblivion, she tumbled arms flailing. Her head struck the sandy bottom. Sharp pain radiated through one temple and bubbles rushed past her eyes spilling precious oxygen from her mouth. Unlike the stories of people drowning at sea, her life did not flash before her eyes, and she had no pangs of regret for a life lost. Instead, a calm descended on her and time slowed. *I'm drowning.*

Above, the once picture-perfect sunny day offered intermittent peaks of light through the swirling sea. Hopes of starting a new life in Florida crowded her mind. Anger flashed, and she would be damned if she would give up and become another statistic. Determination sent a rush of adrenaline flooding through her. *Get your act together, Miss Blake, you did not come this far to die.* Lungs bursting, she pushed straining muscles to the limit to break free of the current and popped up like a cork in the surf. Dragging in great gulps of air, she caught a wave and swum for the beach. Water smashed her dragging her back again. Thinking all was lost, she bobbed helplessly on the surface and then with another loud roar, the merciless sea picked her up and dumped her on the beach. Disorientated, she forced aching limbs to drag her from the water but another wave wrapped like a whip around her legs and she slid helplessly along the shore break.

Grabbing at anything for a handhold, she dug her fingers into the sand. The beach blurred before her and eyes stinging, she blinked wildly at the shadowy figure looming in front of her. Sliding between a pair of long legs, she looped her arms around one muscular calf clinging for dear life. The stranger gripped her arms in his strong hands and lifted her to her feet. Gasping and weak with shock, she stared through a veil of wet hair into the face of the most delicious man she had ever seen in her life. Deep blue eyes shaded by a black Stetson examined her face. *I'm dead and in the arms of a dark angel. Oh, shit, do fallen angels wear black cowboy hats? I might have guessed I would go straight to hell and not pass go.* She turned her head and coughed, spluttering out a mouthful of salt water. When a deep Texan drawl poured over her like warm honey, her knees buckled in relief.

"Hello, darlin'. Don't worry, I have you."

Oh, my God, he's real.

The stranger pulled her against his broad chest and pushed the soaking hair from her face. "You . . . ah, might want to straighten your bikini."

Uncomprehending, she gazed into concerned eyes with dark lashes long enough to make any woman weep. She opened her mouth to speak, but only a squeak emerged. Her rescuer raised one perfect black eyebrow and gave her a wide sexy smile then using one hand, pulled up her bikini pants to cover her bottom.

"Your bikini looks like a full diaper. You'll need to rinse out the sand."

Aware of the grit in her mouth and bits of — dear God — seaweed stuck in her teeth. She tried to speak but her throat constricted in a coughing fit then a loud sneeze exploded from her nostrils. Horrified at the streams of mucus running toward her mouth, she covered her face with both hands and looked around frantically for something to wipe her nose.

Rather than showing disgust the delicious man chuckled, pulled a small packet of tissues from his pocket and handed them to her.

"Don't worry, darlin', getting dumped happens to the best of us." He supported her with a brawny arm wrapped around her waist.

She leaned away, turning her head to clean her face. "I am *so* embarrassed." She balled up the tissues in one hand. "That hasn't happened to me before, and I'm not going near the water again — not ever."

"Don't worry. I'll help you to clean up. I have a bottle of water just over there." He indicated with his chin toward a pile of towels and a guitar sitting on the beach a few feet away. "Before you move, I suggest you cover your . . . ah *breasts*. As much as I find them attractive, you'll get arrested for going topless on this beach."

Suddenly fully aware of warm flesh pressing against her bare freezing and very hard nipples, she glanced down. Her bikini top had ridden up to reveal her to the world. Her face flamed red hot, and she swiftly pushed the swimsuit back into place. She took a step toward the towels, and to her horror, her pants slid down to hang between her legs in a sodden mass. Moments later the stranger wrapped her in a towel and stepped back.

"You might want to wipe the sand from your face. Don't worry about the towel, I have another." He gave her a kind smile. "Where are your clothes? I'll collect them and help you to the public restrooms. They have showers." He broke the seal on a bottle of water then thrust it into her hand. "Rinse out your mouth and spit. Don't swallow the sand."

Taking a sip then turning her back on him to wash away the saline and bits of seaweed trapped between her teeth, she waved a hand in the general direction of her belongings. "My things are over there." She gripped the towel with one hand and pointed to her white daisy patterned beach bag some way away.

"Stay here, and I'll get them for you." He jogged down the sand, six-five of Oh-My-God, bronzed, muscled cowboy.

She stared after him acutely aware of her dripping nose, sand filled pants, and pale English skin. Good heavens, he was the first decent looking man she had actually spoken to under the age of seventy since arriving in Florida, and she resembled a drowned slobbering rat. *I sure know how to make a good impression.* Wishing the ground would open up and swallow her, she mopped at her face. After securing the towel firmly around her waist, she combed fingers through soaked matted hair. Dragging out pieces of seaweed, she moaned in pleasure at the sight of him striding toward her. How could so much delicious be poured into one man? Mesmerized, she watched him bend to push his belongings into a beach bag, sling the guitar over one shoulder, then gripping both bags in one large fist, he offered his arm as if he'd walked straight out of the pages of *Gone with the Wind*.

"I'll help you to the showers." He turned his blue gaze on her and his full lips quirked into a smile. "What's your name, darlin'?"

"Susan, Susie Blake." She gripped his arm and hung on tight to the towel. As they moved slowly toward the restrooms, she became acutely aware of his enticing aftershave.

"Well, nice to meet you, Susie. My name is Branch Durham." He grinned at her mischievously, and she leaned into him glad of his strength. He gave her a long considering look. "Do I detect an English accent?"

"Yes, I'm fresh off the boat from London, and so far my accent is causing difficulties. I tried to communicate with the elderly people in my building, but it doesn't matter they all took off in a hurry early this morning."

"Well, I understand you fine, darlin', and I *love* your accent." He chuckled when she gaped at him in surprise. "But you do have the sea change crowd here. With retired people from different states, I guess some of them would have trouble understanding me too."

"Oh, I see. We have different accents in the UK as well. In fact, in London alone, if you walk across the river many of the people have a different accent. I feel out of place here which is ridiculous as I was born in Boston."

A slow smile lifted the corners of his mouth.

"Boston? Well, don't that beat all?" His gaze drifted over her face and rested on her lips before returning to her eyes. "You sure look like an English rose to me. I wouldn't mind betting your mom is English, and you favor her."

Pushing a lock of wet hair behind one ear and doing her best to act nonchalant, she offered him a small smile. He must be very shortsighted to believe she resembled anything close to beautiful with seaweed clinging to her face and sand filling her pants.

Perhaps he was just being nice. She fell into his gaze. How easy he had cast his spell over her. Did she care? Hell no. His oh, so handsome features and sexy accent sent quivers of awareness along every nerve ending. *Oh boy, you are gorgeous.* "Funnily enough I *do* resemble my mother."

When he lifted an eyebrow as if in question, she decided to offer him a brief explanation of why she settled in Florida. "When my parents divorced, my mother returned to the UK with me, hence the accent." She glanced up at him. Something about him was strangely familiar but how could she forget meeting a man who looked like him. She cleared her throat forcing her mind from her delicious companion to concentrate. "Recently, my mother remarried, and my father offered me the opportunity to manage his apartment building, so I left the freezing winters in London for the Florida sunshine."

"I prefer the sunshine too." Branch's mouth quirked up into a lopsided smile. "Have the tenants accepted you as your father's replacement?"

"That's difficult to judge as I only arrived yesterday." She shrugged. "I didn't expect to have a problem communicating with them. This is a real problem for me because they're scared of the hurricane. I have no idea what to tell them, and the weatherman didn't say anything about evacuating the area." She shrugged, realizing she had probably not fully understood the gravity of the situation. "Before breakfast this morning, most of the condos had their blinds down, and the residents had packed their cars to leave. Of course, I've seen the damage caused by storms in this part of the world, but I assumed the local news channel and the radio would issue warnings if the danger were imminent."

"Yeah, they do, and I guess it depends on where you're living. I wouldn't want to be in a ground floor apartment in case of flooding. I live high up, and in the middle of my building and of course, I have a good supply of fresh water and canned goods in case I'm isolated for a long period of time." Branch led her toward the entrance of the amenities block. "You do understand there's the potential the buildings could be completely demolished in a hurricane of this magnitude?"

This magnitude? She stepped away and catching the seriousness of his expression turned to face him. "Yes, of course, but I spoke to my father before he left for his honeymoon in Hawaii. He told me he had built the condominiums to withstand hurricanes after one destroyed the last building he owned. All the windows in our building have metal shutters. In fact, my father insists the building could withstand an earthquake too."

"That sounds like my place. Well, it used to be my dad's condo, but I kept it because it's peaceful here and I like the quiet." Branch waved toward the opening to the amenities block. "Can you manage from here?"

She gave him a long lingering look. At least she had met one good-looking man around her own age and considering everyone else in her building had retired, life was certainly looking up. Although, she doubted she would ever set eyes on this gorgeous hunk again. He had been kind to help, but from his expression, it was obvious he had no plans to stick around, and she could not blame him, she resembled a beached whale. Offering her hand, she smiled up at him. "I can't thank you enough for saving my life."

"Anytime, darlin'." Branch flashed her a set of perfect white teeth and tipped his hat then rather than shaking her hand, he handed over her bag. "As we're probably the only two young people left in the area, would you consider meeting me at the coffee shop across the road in say half an hour? They haven't closed up and run for the hills yet." His gaze drifted over her again. "Or do you need more time?"

Her face grew hot, and she stared at her sand-caked feet. "Thank you, that would be lovely, and half an hour is more than enough time." She pointed to the building opposite the beach road. "I live across the street — over there. The coffee shop is in front of my building."

"I'm right next door." He grinned and tipped his hat then strolled toward the coffee shop.

She stared after him taking in his broad shoulders and long muscular legs. He moved with athletic grace, his white western shirt, embroidered with guitars, billowed out behind him with each step, showing an alluring expanse of tanned muscular back. Realizing she was taking up precious minutes ogling the delicious cowboy, she turned and ran into the showers. Diving into her bag for her toiletries, she calculated the time needed to dash home, dry her hair, and apply a little makeup before meeting him. Moving like a woman possessed, she washed her hair, dressed, and dashed in the direction of her condominium. Once inside, she changed into a pair of white capris and a blue cotton blouse, dried her hair, and applied a minimum of makeup. Taking a quick glance in the mirror, she picked up her keys and headed downstairs.

Branch placed his guitar on a seat then buttoned up his shirt before sitting at one of the tables inside the coffee shop. After avoiding going into stores since his arrival, he cringed when the server recognized him immediately. Patting her bleached blonde hair, she walked toward him notepad and pencil in hand. He smiled at her. "I guess you'll be closing soon with the storm bearing down on us?"

"Dave is packing up as we speak, but I'm sure we'll have time to serve *you,* Mr. Durham. I loved your last album. I play it all the time." She offered him her order pad. "Could I get an autograph? Can you make it out to 'my friend Clarice'?"

He raised a brow and gave her his best smile. "Now, darlin', what would that do to my reputation? We've only just met."

He took the pen and pad then scrawled "To Clarice from Branch Durham" and handed it back to her glad to see she peeled off the slip of paper and pushed it inside her pocket. The last thing he wanted was Susie discovering his life was part of the fame game. For once in his career as a world-famous Country and Western singer, he had met a woman who had no idea who he was or what he did for a living. The singing career aside, his family owned Durham Oil, which made him and his brothers the constant targets of gold digging women. The ten minutes spent with Susie had been as refreshing as a spring breeze.

Of late, he had lost interest in women in general. None of them could see past the fame or millions to the simple man underneath. At first, it was flattering when women constantly offered him their bodies, but lately, he hated being nothing more than a sex object, and that image did nothing to help his creativity. Sure, he planned a future with a wife, kids, and a white picket fence but the models or film stars he dated would not be happy on a ranch. He wanted a normal, uncomplicated sweet girl for his wife. He smiled at the memory of Susie pressed against him, her hard, pink nipples topped nice natural breasts, and she sure felt good in his arms, soft, feminine, not the muscular women with fake tits and tan that usually ended up in his bed. He rubbed his chin. How strange a woman covered with sand and seaweed had grabbed his attention. His attraction toward her had been immediate, and the need to protect her had shocked him. He had to find out more about her and maybe enjoy being normal for once.

What if she's married? He stared out the window and grinned. *What is she's not?*

It was a disaster waiting to happen. He preferred honesty but desperately wanted to keep his fame from her. She appeared too nice for him, and his notoriety with women would likely frighten her away. Sidestepping any questions about his successful music career would be better than lying to her. Better, if she figured he was a beach bum, then she would act normally in front of him. He smiled at Clarice. "I'll order in a moment. I'm waiting for a friend." To his relief, the door swung open to reveal his little mermaid. "There she is now." He lifted a hand and waved to Susie to join him.

"You made it in fifteen minutes." As she reached the table with her hair mussed up from the howling wind, he stood and pulled out a chair for her. "You sure are a pretty little thing. It was hard to tell under all the sand." He grinned then noticed her cheeks pink with embarrassment.

Oh Lord, from her downcast gaze and painfully obvious embarrassment, she did not have too much experience with men. *How old are you honey?* Panic of the media photographing him with an underage half-naked girl washed over him. He could imagine the vicious mileage they would make out of ruining his career over nothing. *I'm in a restaurant, in public. It's all good.* He sat opposite her to keep an appropriate distance then cleared his throat and motioned toward the server. "What would you like to eat? The apple pie here is legendary, so my dad informed me."

"Apple pie and coffee would be wonderful thank you." Susie looked at him from below her lashes.

"I'll have the same." He winked at the server and waited until she sashayed away before turning back to Susie. "I must apologize for being so rude before, ma'am. My grandma would whoop my ass for speaking to a fine lady like that although I did mean the comment respectfully. You *are* a natural beauty, and these days that's hard to find." He ignored the desire to cup her chin and make her look at him. "I guess you're not used to the rough edges of a cowboy?"

When she lifted her cornflower blue eyes to him, his heart skipped a beat.

"I didn't think you were rude, but it will take me some time to get used to the laid-back lifestyle here." The tips of her ears turned a delightful shade of crimson. "Where I lived in London, it was . . . well, a little formal and, I'm not used to compliments, especially from strangers."

Oh, Jesus, you are young. He wondered if anyone had noticed him on the beach holding her delightful breasts against his chest. Although only a few people had ventured onto the sand, he had no doubt all of them would be carrying cell phones with excellent cameras. Scandal of that type would ruin his career. He had to work out a way to discover her age without asking her outright. Playing with the sugar bowl, he flicked her a glance. "That's a very unworldly thing to say. I'm sure you had plenty of admirers at college."

"I went to university in London, but I didn't have much time to think about boys." Susie let out a long sigh. "My father might own property here, but he didn't offer me or my mother any assistance. I attended classes during the day and waited tables at night. It was a very long, hard four years."

Thank you, Jesus. "So what changed his mind?"

"His interest in me increased once I turned twenty-one and obtained my business degree. I am also a qualified accountant, so now I'm very useful to him." She met his gaze with a small smile. "Then he announced he was remarrying and offered me the position of running his building here in Florida. The last I heard he'd purchased a house in Hawaii and doesn't intend to return anytime soon, so if the building survives the hurricane it looks like I'll have a permanent position."

Smart and beautiful. "Didn't your father meet you at the airport?"

"No, he'd left before I arrived. He'd sent me a letter with instructions and the keys to his car and condo." She giggled, and he noticed her cheeks dimpling. "Can you imagine the trouble I had trying to drive a Cadillac? You see for me it has the steering wheel on the left instead of the right, and you drive on the wrong side of the road." She raised her eyebrows at his frown. "We drive on the left-hand side in the UK. Add the fact I had no idea which direction to go. My car at home has satellite navigation but not my dad's 1963 Cadillac."

Suppressing a grin and trying hard not to laugh, he forced his brow into a frown. "So, what did you do? You obviously arrived here in the end."

"I ended up asking a cab driver if I could follow him here." She grinned widely showing a set of perfect white teeth. "He thought I was some crazy English woman but accepted. I might add the car is staying in the parking lot from now on. The drive here took ten years off my life."

He chuckled. "I bet it did." He took his cell phone from his pocket. "I'll get an update on the storm." He waited for the page to load and frowned. "It looks like it won't be anywhere near here until late this afternoon."

The server came back with two cups of coffee and large slices of apple pie *a la mode.* He thanked her before turning his attention back to Susie. He wanted time to get to know her and chatting in a coffee shop would be nice and safe. "So, what do you remember about your time in Boston?"

After some coaxing, Susie gave him her life story, and they chatted like old friends. He managed to sidestep most of the questions about his life and luckily other than refilling their coffee cups his fan had kept her distance.

"Do you miss Texas?" Susie tossed her blonde hair over one shoulder. "I assume by your accent your home is in that state." She lifted a fork full of apple pie and held it hovering in midair above her plate.

He pushed a hand through his hair and decided to give her an abridged version of his life. He wanted her to know him as a simple man. He would leave out his wealthy oil baron heritage and the cattle ranch. He dare not mention his songwriting and recording fame. "Sometimes but it's only a short flight away." He inclined his head and racked his brain to come up with a plausible excuse for not having a job. "Some years ago, my pa gave his ranch to me and my brothers and then purchased a condo here to retire. He died a few months back, in fact almost one year to the date we lost our mom, and I moved in to sort out his affairs."

"I'm so sorry." Susie's cute face creased into a frown. "Tell me about your brothers. I guess they're at home running the ranch?"

"Yeah, the eldest two oversee the running of the ranch but the eldest works in Dallas most of the time and my younger brother is at college. They're doing fine with Grandma Durham keeping an eye on them." He wanted to leave his story there, but something inside him wanted to share his life with her. "I have a place of my own right next door, and I have a few head of cattle, but my love is horses."

"So I gather you prefer to be on your own?" Susie wet her succulent lips. "So are your brothers running your place as well at the moment?"

"Ah, I'm rarely alone. There are many hands working on my ranch, and I have a great manager taking care of the place. I'm often away more than home of late." He sighed remembering the time before he became famous. "I used to enjoy doing the rodeo circuit, but since Pa died, I don't have the time." *Because I'm on tour or writing songs most of the year.*

"No, I don't imagine you do if you're in charge of your father's estate." She reached across the table and squeezed his hand. "He would be proud of you. I'm sure he is looking down on you and smiling — and you saved my life. You get extra points for doing that you know."

The warmth from her hand and compassionate gaze made his stomach squeeze. She had the power to captivate with a look and had no notion of her effect on men. A song drifted into his mind, and he stared at her in disbelief. Perhaps the lyrics he had written about recognizing a soulmate by the look in her eyes had been true after all.

Swallowing the emotional lump in his throat, he turned over his hand and linked their fingers. The action seemed natural as if they were lovers. He blinked. *Oh shit, don't go and get all misty.* "Thank you. That's a lovely thing to say." He shrugged. "I feel him looking over my shoulder sometimes and saying, 'the best things in life are worth waiting for.' He often said that to me." He smiled at her wistful expression. "Damned if I know what he meant."

"You should have listened to him." She slipped another forkful of pie between her lips and sighed. "Your father was a sensible man and one of good taste. This pie is delicious."

Her giggle broke the tension, and he reached for his coffee glad of the respite. They chatted for hours before the shop owner made a great show of winding down the shutters and giving him a meaningful stare. *It must be time to leave.* He glanced out the door and frowned. The storm was closing in faster than expected. A gust of wind buffeted the building making the colorful canvas awnings flap wildly, and dust devils of sand danced along the sidewalk. He stared at a bank of storm clouds building on the horizon. He had been in Florida during a hurricane and understood how fast a storm cell of this size could move. Although his father had built the condominiums to withstand high winds, nothing was certain when dealing with Mother Nature.

In an attempt to offer reassurance to Susie, he indicated with his chin toward the dark sky. "The storm is moving down the coast and if you have elderly people in your building requiring assistance to catch the bus to the shelter we should hurry along as soon as possible. I'm staying because by now the roads will be jammed with traffic and I don't want to be caught out in the open in my car."

"I have nowhere else to go, so I'm staying too." Susie smiled at the server stacking chairs. "I think most of the residents in my building left earlier, but I agree some may need my help. My father gave me a brief idea of what managing his building consisted of, but he didn't mention what to do during a hurricane. I guess it's much the same as any storm?" She sipped her drink then ran the tip of her pink tongue across her full bottom lip.

Mesmerized by the innocent wetting of her lips, Branch cleared his throat. "Hurricanes are more than just a storm. Do you have provisions in case we're isolated for a long time? Bottled water, a portable gas stove, flashlight, batteries, and food to see you through a couple of weeks if necessary?"

"I'm not sure. I'll have to check the cupboards." She glanced out the door and grimaced. "I hate storms, and that one is moving so fast. It looks terrifying."

Branch sucked in a deep breath. "I know we only met today, but if it gets bad out there, you're welcome to sit out the storm with me." He grinned and crossed his heart. "I swear I'm not an ax murderer, but if it makes you feel comfortable, I don't have a problem if you carry a gun."

The fear in her eyes froze the grin on his lips. He leaned back in the chair and lifted his coffee cup observing her over the rim. Had he said something inappropriate again? When Susie lifted her gaze to him again. He offered her a smile. "Did I put my foot in it again?"

"No . . . apart from the gun thing. I've not handled a weapon in my life. In fact, I think I would panic if I saw one up close." She lifted her cup, sipped then met his gaze. "It's not usual for people to own guns in the UK."

He held up both hands. "I didn't know. I'm sorry."

"It's okay and thank you for the offer. It's nice to know I have somewhere to go if it gets crazy outside." Her smile lit up her eyes. "I'm a good judge of character, and I would enjoy your company. Although, I'll most likely have to stay in my apartment because I'm committed to keeping an eye out for the residents if any of them decide to remain in the building."

"I'll have to check to see who is left in my building as well." He leaned back in his chair and rubbed his chin. "In my building, they leave their names on a chalkboard in the recreation room, so we know if they have left or are staying."

"My father didn't mention much about his tenants. Is that the usual practice?" Susie frowned. "I tried to call him earlier but got a message saying he didn't want to be disturbed."

What an asshole. "I've no idea what people do in your building, so we'll do a door knock and ask someone. If they don't have an evacuation plan, we'll check on everyone in your building." He pushed his cup away. "Looking at the way the wind has picked up I don't think we have too much time to get everything squared away and I'm sure the folks here want to close up. I'll go back to my building and make sure my place is secure and then I'll come over and help you." He smiled.

"Thank you." Susie beamed at him. "I'll check on supplies and meet you in the foyer." She picked up her purse and pulled out some notes. "My treat." She placed the notes on the table, got to her feet, and headed for the door.

Branch stared after her speechless. He could not remember how long it had been since anyone had bought *him* a meal. He grinned and reached for the Stetson hanging over the back of the chair. With his hat placed firmly on his head, guitar under one arm, he picked up his bag and headed toward his building then stopped to check on Susie's progress. Ahead, she moved slowly toward the glass door of her building, keeping close to the wall with her clothes flapping in the wind. He wondered how she was keeping her balance. He heaved a sigh of relief to see her slip through the entrance. With every step toward his building, powerful gusts of wind battered his back pushing him forward. He glanced over one shoulder and picked up his pace. The hurricane had intensified and was heading toward the coast at an incredible pace. Dark clouds whipped across the sky and the horizon bubbled in a disturbing shade of purple gray. *Oh, shit.*

CHAPTER TWO

Susie pulled the keys from her purse and moved swiftly toward the control panel on the wall beside the fire alarm. Searching for the correct key took longer than she anticipated, but finally, a key slotted into the lock and the shutters on the glass front of the building slid down and clicked into place. The single shutter covering the front door she could utilize manually once she had some idea if the tenants had decided to stay or leave. Heading for the elevator, she stepped inside and punched the number for the penthouse apartment. Riding up she thought about the conversation with Branch. She had willingly divulged her life story almost down to the color of her panties, but he had only given her a brief outline of his. She had no inkling if he had a girlfriend or a wife living with him. He hadn't mentioned either but how could a man that good-looking *not* have someone special? *Perhaps he's gay.* She smiled. *Yes, a compassionate gay man would be nice to me and have no ulterior motive.*

The elevator doors slid open in the hallway of her apartment, and she stepped inside the opulent sitting room. Her attention went to the palm tree leaves sticking to the front windows opposite the beach. Long rivulets of water streamed down the glass, and an eerie roll of thunder sounded in the distance. She ran to the control panel and deployed the shutters then reached for the light switch. The items Branch mentioned she required to survive the storm should be stored somewhere. Standing in the middle of the room, she gazed in all directions searching for a large storage area of some kind. "Well Susie, my dear, it looks like you'll have to open every damn cupboard."

Dropping her purse onto the nearest chair, she headed down the hallway. Opening the first door, which happened to be her father's old bedroom, she opened the closet and found nothing but a few lonely shirts hanging from the pole. Her father had given her the combination to the wall safe set in the back of the cupboard and made her aware of the pistol and ammunition inside. Her skin crawled at the idea of a weapon within reach, and she hurried out the door. She moved swiftly from room to room and found nothing of use. Determined to find her father's supplies, she made her way into the large galley kitchen. On her arrival, she found the cupboards, fridge, and freezer well stocked with food but had not noticed large quantities of anything in particular. The kitchen had a pantry containing the usual canned goods and bottles of homemade preserves obviously given to her father by some of his tenants. She scanned the shelves then bent to examine a row of fitted cupboards running the length of each wall beneath the shelves. Kneeling on the floor, she slid back the first door and peered inside. An immense feeling of relief flooded over her. Boxes of provisions, water, batteries, and other essentials filled every nook and cranny.

Pushing to her feet, she selected one of the flashlights, checked if it worked, then collected a packet of batteries and returned to the kitchen. She glanced at the clock. Searching the apartment had taken longer than she had anticipated. Sliding the keys into the pocket of her capris, she headed for the door. After stepping inside the elevator, she realized the danger of a power failure, trapping her inside and her heart raced. Once the car reached the ground floor, she let out a sigh of relief. The doors opened to reveal Branch leaning against the wall. She caught her breath at the sight of the wet shirt clinging to his impressive six-pack and the jeans clinging to his long legs and slim hips like snakeskin. Raindrops glistened on his black cowboy hat and sprinkled the hair curling at his nape. The sight of his wet muscular body sent tingles of awareness straight to her pussy. He was sex on a stick, and she had a craving to lick him all over. Oh, boy, if he wasn't gay then he had player written all over him, but for once in her dull life, she did not give a damn.

She straightened and pushing down the nagging voice in the back of her mind to be careful of strangers, strolled from the elevator. The smile he gave her filled her with confidence as if she had known him forever. When he tipped his hat, and his Texan drawl flowed over her, all her doubts about him vanished.

"Well, darlin', you're the first woman who hasn't kept me waiting."

So not gay then. "I *am* aware of the urgency of our current situation." Her face heated. "The good news is I *do* have supplies and enough food and water to last two weeks at least."

"Great!" Branch pushed away from the wall and strolled toward her. "I noticed your tenants have posted a list on the notice board. I think they have all left the building and most of them have given contact details. I assume your apartment number is twenty-five? That's the only one without a name attached."

She nodded. "Yes, that's me." Her attention moved past him to the wind whipping sand and leaves against the front door. "It's getting crazy out there. I've no idea what to do in a hurricane. Can you give me some advice?"

Branch gave her a slow, sexy smile.

"Sure." He indicated toward the elevator with his chin. "If you plan to go upstairs make it quick and stay in one place. Keep away from the windows. Worst case scenario, the roof peels off, and as you're on the top floor, it might be a problem if access to the fire stairs is blocked." He shrugged. "My place is in the middle, and I have plenty of supplies and three bedrooms. Like I said before, you are welcome to come over and stay at my place for the duration."

Let me see, stay in this building alone and scared out of my wits or move in with a handsome cowboy. Decisions, decisions. She nodded in agreement. "Thank you, that would be wonderful. I really appreciate the offer, but I'll need to risk the elevator again to pick up my bags. Luckily I haven't unpacked all my things yet."

"Okay, but make it fast." Branch strolled toward the elevator and pressed the button. "I caught the weather report on TV before I came over and the storm might just brush this part of the coast, but hurricanes are known to change direction without warning, so it's better to be safe than sorry."

Ten minutes later, Susie followed him out into the pouring rain. When Branch took one of her bags then offered his hand, she took it and dragging a suitcase on wheels behind her followed him slowly toward his building. Wind whipped sand into her face, and the blasts tore at her skin like sandpaper. She fought for each step against the ferocious wind and without Branch's hand as an anchor the wind would have blown her over. Panic welled up in an uncontrollable rush. She fought for breath and cried out in fear. The next moment, Branch had pressed her against his hard chest and nestled under his arm as they staggered toward his building. Once inside, she stepped away embarrassed, but he moved closer enclosing her with his warm, masculine scent then pushed the soaking hair from her face, and cupped her chin in one large hand.

"Don't worry, darlin', I won't let anything happen to you. Cross my heart."

She stared into his eyes and forced her trembling lips into a smile. "Thank you. I've not experienced a storm like this before. I'm sorry for acting like an idiot."

"There's nothing wrong with being scared. A hurricane isn't something to take lightly." He placed her bag on the floor then turned away to pull down the shutters before speaking to an elderly couple waiting in the foyer.

"It would be best if you stayed inside your apartment." Branch smiled at the old man. "Do you want me to come up and secure your shutters?"

"That's all taken care of thank you, Branch." The old man held out his hand. "You're a good boy, and your father would be proud of you staying here to take care of us old folks, when you should be out kicking up your heels."

"Why, thank you, Mr. Smithers." Branch shook his hand and smiled at the elderly gray-haired woman beside him. "It's good to see you again, ma'am. Don't forget now, if you need help just give me a call. The intercom works on batteries, so you'll be able to contact me in a blackout."

Mrs. Smithers gripped Branch's arm, her pale age marked skin and thin fingers a stark contrast against his healthy suntanned flesh.

"Thank you. Bert is unable to drive anymore, so we'll have to wait this one out." She turned to Susie and smiled. "You're lucky to have found Branch. He cared for his father right to the end, and not many sons would give up their career to live here with us elderly folk."

"I am lucky. He rescued me from drowning earlier." Susie smiled to cover the fear prickling her skin. Wind shook the metal roll down shutters and bits of trembling greenery stuck through every tiny gap. Before she could offer the old lady a reply, Branch took her hand, picked up her bag, and led her toward the elevator. When he winked at her then turned and grinned at Mrs. Smithers, her stomach gave a strange twist of pleasure.

"There you go again, matchmaking." Branch chuckled. "Susie here is Max Blake's daughter. He'd have my hide if I didn't look out for his little girl."

She frowned. "I didn't know you'd met my father."

"I haven't, but I do know he owns the building next door."

The elevator doors slid shut, and he dropped her hand to depress a button on the panel. When he gazed down at her, the desire to melt into his strong arms forced her to look away. As if reading her mind, he cleared his throat.

"You'll be safe with me." Branch grinned and shook his head. "Dear Lord, I guess a serial killer would say the same thing, but really, I don't go where I'm not wanted." The silver doors opened, and he led her down a passageway and stopped at a door.

"Welcome to my humble abode." He dug into his pocket for a set of keys then opened the door. "Make yourself at home."

The moment she stepped inside, she caught a concentrated version of his unique scent and bit back a purr. His musky aftershave had infused the tidy, comfortable apartment and she wanted to roll in it. *Get a grip. This handsome cowboy isn't interested in me. He is just being neighborly.* She dragged her bag behind her, and of course, the wheels had to squeak as if she had filled the bag with rats. Following him into a spacious sitting room, through an open plan kitchen, and down a hallway, she kept her head down not wanting to appear nosy. The next moment she hit a wall of muscle, staggered back, tripped over her bag and sat down heavily legs sprawled. "Oops." *Now he thinks I'm an idiot as well as stupid.* She took the hand he offered and scrambled to her feet noticing the amusement in his eyes.

"Are you hurt?" Branch's mouth quivered on the edge of a grin.

She pulled down her shirt then pushed the hair from her eyes. "I'm fine."

To her relief, he ignored her burning cheeks, pushed open a door, and flicked on the lights.

"This is your room." He dropped her bag inside and gave her a smile that would have most women swooning. "I'll put on a pot of coffee then go and get out of these wet clothes. I suggest you do the same. There are plenty of fresh towels in the bathroom cupboard. Then, I guess we'd better turn on the news and see which way this storm is heading."

She leaned against the wall, and her attention fixed on his long stride and the way his wet clothes hugged his impressive physique. Oh boy, he was just as good walking away. Closing the door, she turned the lock then peeled off her soaking clothes. Shaking with cold and being naked in a stranger's apartment was bad enough but the sudden gunshot splatter of hail on the shutters terrified her. She dashed into the bathroom and turned on the hot shower. The storm had intensified, and she might not have the luxury in a few hours. Fear hurried her along, and in less than ten minutes, she had finished and dressed. A crack of lightning followed by a roll of thunder pushed her heart rate into overdrive, and she turned for the door. Before she had taken one step the lights flickered and went out plunging the room into darkness. Lightning strobed making the room flicker like an old silent movie. Disorientated, she stumbled into the nightstand. Pain shot through her hip, and she cried out. Strong gusts of wind rattled the shutters conjuring images of demons slipping through the cracks to grab her. Choking back sobs of fear, she ran one hand along the wall seeking the door. *I have to get out of here.*

"Damn." Branch pulled out his cell phone and activated the inbuilt light. He located the lantern and switched it on then turned toward the coffee pot and sighed with relief. "At least the coffee is ready."

His mind went to the young woman in his spare bedroom, and he wet his lips. *She sure is a pretty little thing.* Usually, he preferred his women tall, skinny, and brunette but man, after having Susie in his arms his preferences had made a one-eighty-degree turn. Add her oh, so sweet innocent expression, her fascinating accent, and she flew up to the top of his "girls I want to date" list with a bullet. He rubbed his chin and stared down the hallway toward her room. At first, he figured her innocence was an act, but the way she reacted to him had changed his mind. Susie was not at all worldly, and although obviously smart, he gathered the trip to Florida was her first try at independence. He had to admit her clumsy self-consciousness was kind of cute and brought out his need to protect her. The problem was, he had experienced firsthand the way women changed the moment they discovered his celebrity status. Clingy, demanding women, he did not need or those looking to take him for his fortune. Although, he had not sensed that trait in Susie. She intrigued him, so he would make sure to take it slow with her.

Lightning flashed, and the windows shook from the immediate rolls of thunder. Deafened by the noise of hail striking the metal shutters, he strolled toward Susie's room and stopped outside her door. His stomach dropped at the sound of her sobs. "Hey, Susie, open the door. I have a flashlight and hot coffee." Holy cow, she really was terrified of storms, and this one had barely started.

The door handle squeaked, and Susie ran to him flinging trembling arms around his neck. Trying to avoid his natural reaction to a sexy young woman's hard nipples pressed against his chest, he bit back a groan and rubbed her back. "It's going be fine. The storm isn't as close as it sounds." He reluctantly peeled her trembling body away, turned her around, and pushed her toward the kitchen. "I have a radio. Even in a blackout we'll be able to listen to the latest information." He pulled out a chair to the kitchen table. "Sit down, and I'll get the coffee. I have a thermos bottle for the rest, so we can have it later if we don't have power."

"I'm dreadfully afraid of storms." Susie sank into the chair and gripped the table. Her eyes flicked constantly to the windows. With each roll of thunder, her face paled, and terror etched her face. "Have you heard any more news?"

Acting as nonchalantly as possible to calm her, he poured the coffee and sat opposite. "Not yet and the server is down so I can't check on my cell phone. Cream and sugar?" He waved at the two containers on the table. "I'll turn on the radio but the lightning interferes with reception and I'm worried the crackling might upset you more than you are now."

"I'd rather know what's happening out there." Susie gave him a quivering smile then let go of the table long enough to add cream and sugar to her coffee. "I'm sure a few crackles on the radio couldn't possibly make it any worse." She stirred the coffee slowly flinching each time another flash of lightning lit up the room.

He lifted the radio from the counter and switched it on selecting a news channel. A crackling voice came through the speakers

"Here is an update on the tropical storm watch for the east-central Florida coast. Hurricane Ziggy's center is moving north with maximum winds of fifty miles per hour with winds extending seventy miles from its center. Conditions are likely to deteriorate as the storm moves northward over the next few hours. The Hurricane Center is urging all residents from Fort Pierce to Flagler Beach to evacuate. Those who leave should follow orders from local officials. Don't forget to let friends and family know where you are, folks. Stay tuned. I'll be broadcasting the latest weather updates and emergency instructions every thirty minutes. In the meantime, sit back and listen to 'Comin' Home'—"

Branch accidentally knocked the radio from the bench in an attempt to prevent the announcer mentioning his name as the singer of his latest hit single. He juggled the radio in one hand, managing to switch it off before it hit the ground. Straightening he glanced at Susie who was watching him with an astonished expression on her face. He offered her a smile. "I think the storm is making me a little jumpy too." Dang, his face had grown hot. Holy cow, he hadn't blushed since high school.

"Oh, I thought the idea of listening to country music had you moving fast to change the channel." She inclined her head to one side and examined his face closely. "Funny, you come over as all cowboy to me. Not that I've ever met one before, but we do have the pseudo-Cowboys in England. They meet each week, and boot scoot the night away and even have line dancing competitions. It's really funny to listen to a cowboy with a cockney accent." She grinned, and her eyes twinkled with mischief. "You look like the real deal, and your accent is pure country."

How am I going to get myself out of this one? Branch lifted his cup to his lips to give him time to consider a reply. He refused to lie to her so he would have to come up with an excuse to slip around the edges of the truth. He took a sip, enjoying the rich taste flowing across his tongue and sighed. "Oh, I *love* Country and Western music." He leaned back in the chair and stretched out his legs to appear nonchalant. "I was just saving the batteries." He glanced at his watch. "I'll turn it on again in half an hour to catch the next report." Feeling happy with his excuse, he took another sip of his coffee and eyed her over the rim.

"I don't really like country music at all." Susie frowned then stared into her cup. "Not that I've kept up with the current hits, but I hate the old stuff. The 'I'm sad because my dog died and my truck broke down' songs. I *mean*, cowboys can't look after their dogs very well if they're continually dropping dead." She snorted with laughter. "I think I can name ten songs about some poor kid having to shoot his old dog or the dog has been hit by a truck. I would think there would be more to sing about in the country than dogs and trucks."

He placed his cup on the table and raised a brow. "Yeah, I can see your point, but my taste leans more toward songs about sunsets and love. There are some beautiful lyrics written about lost love or the one that got away in every musical genre." He took a deep breath and let it out on a sigh. "My particular favorite is country rock, but I must admit I like a good ballad."

"I noticed your guitar on the beach, so I gather you play?"

"Yeah, I've had that guitar since I was twelve." He grinned at her. "Sitting on an empty beach and singing into the wind has become a pastime of mine for the last few weeks."

A series of lightning strikes lit up the room, and as the thunder boomed, Susie dove under the kitchen table and gripped his legs like a boa constrictor. With her trembling body wrapped around him and her face pressed against his thigh, he stroked her hair in an effort to comfort her. "It's only thunder, it's lightning that does the damage, and by the time you hear it, the threat is over." He untangled her hands from around his knees and lifted her onto his lap. "Look at me, Susie. It's going to be okay. The storm is some miles away and may miss us all together."

Unconvinced, Susie slipped her arms around his neck and held on tight. The building shook with every roll of thunder. Another peel of hailstones splattered the shutters and terrified she buried her face in his neck. Her next breath could be her last, but she could not think of a better place to be. When his arms came around her in a comforting hug, instead of instinctively pulling away, she snuggled closer.

"Oh, darlin', if you keep wiggling around like that, I'm not going to be responsible for my actions." Branch pressed kisses across her cheek. "You don't know what you're doing to me, babe."

Oh, she had some idea by the hard length pressing against her hip. She pulled back and gazed into his face. God help her his sexy hooded eyes sent erotic images bouncing around her brain. Dragging her mind firmly away from the thought of being naked under or over his hot, muscular body, she chewed on her bottom lip. "I do know, and although it was unintentional, I'll take it as a compliment."

"My pleasure." Branch eased her away from his groin, and a slow sexy smile curled his lips. "If you keep this up, I think I'm going to like protecting you from the storm."

Realization of his meaning slammed into her. *Now he thinks I sleep around.* "I'll admit I'm scared, but I don't usually act like a sex-starved lunatic. In fact, I've been called frigid by more than one man I've dated, but why should I be expected to go to bed with a man just because he buys me dinner?"

"Oh, darlin', like I said before, I don't go where I'm not wanted, and if I remember rightly, you paid for *my* meal." He grinned and reached for the radio. "I'd better see if there is an update on the storm."

The radio crackled with each flash of lightning, and if the announcer had reported anything new, she could not hear it through the static. She leaned against him and did not intend to move from Branch's lap any time soon. The solid strength of him enclosing her soothed her fear, as did the steady beat of his heart pounding against her ear. When the intercom on the wall beside the front door chimed, and Branch lifted her gently from his lap, she moaned at the loss of him.

"I'll have to answer that, it's probably the old folks you met in the lobby." Branch strolled from the kitchen and across the sitting room to pick up the phone. "Branch Durham." He frowned and turned a concerned gaze in her direction. "I'll come straight down, but I'll have to use the fire escape, so it will take a few minutes before I get there. Close the door to that room and keep away from the windows." He hung up the handset and turned to her. "They need me to secure a window. I shouldn't be too long." He placed one hand on the doorknob. "Stay in your bedroom and take the survival packs with you." He pointed to two stuffed backpacks leaning against the wall. "It's the safest place the bedrooms face away from the sea."

Terrified of being alone, she jumped to her feet and dashed across the room. "I'm not staying here on my own. I'm coming with you."

"No. Stay here, it's safer." He walked toward her, cupped her chin, and brushed her lips with a slow, soft but oh, so sexy kiss. "I'll be back, and it will be quicker if I go alone."

Stunned by the intense touch of his lips, she stared at him in disbelief. Before she could complain, he slipped out the door and headed for the fire stairs. Another clap of thunder rattled the windows and leaving the front door open, she dashed into the dark bedroom. She wanted to hide under the blankets but her shirt stuck to her sweat-soaked skin. Without the air conditioning, the temperature inside the apartment had risen unbearably, and the room had become humid and stuffy. Unable to face the darkness alone, she moved back into the kitchen, sat at the table, and stared out the front door to the deserted passage. The minutes ticked by slowly and with no sign of Branch's return, she tried the radio again. Between the crackles from the lightning strikes, she could make out the presenter's voice giving the hurricane warnings. Unfamiliar with the local landmarks, nothing he said made sense until he mentioned her suburb. The interference from the storm blocked out the warning, but from the way the wind buffeted the building any fool would understand the storm was crossing the coastline.

It came hard, with the roar of a freight train heading toward her. Terrified and unable to move, Susie gripped the edge of the table. As objects smashed into the side of the building, loud bangs echoed through the room and vibrated the floor beneath her feet. She wanted to run away, go anywhere to hide from the storm but fear froze her legs. *Don't just sit here do something, you idiot.* Heart pounding with fear, she grasped the survival packs Branch had mentioned and stared out the open door hoping he would appear. The next moment, a window in the hallway exploded in a shower of glass and metal. Survival instinct took hold, and she ran across the room, along the hallway then dashed into the bedroom. Teeth chattering with fear, she slid under the bed, clutching the survival packs to her chest. *Someone up there is definitely trying to kill me. Twice in one day? Give me a break.*

CHAPTER THREE

B ranch went to check the front doors of his building and found an old couple sheltering inside. "Do you want to come upstairs and wait out the storm with me?"

"No thank you." The old man waved him away. "There is a bus to the shelter due here any moment."

"Okay. I'll wait with you and give you a hand." He stared outside at the driving rain and caught sight of a pair of headlights. "Here it is now."

At the loud honking of a horn, he headed outside into the storm and waved at the bus moving slowly toward his building. The vehicle slowed to a stop, and the doors swished open.

"We've got room for two more, but I can't wait too long the hurricane is almost on us."

Branch turned and waved to the old couple. "Take them."

The bus driver turned a worried expression to Branch and frowned.

"Do you have a friend or family member further inland you can get to and wait out the storm?"

Branch helped the old couple staggering under bags of supplies into the packed bus. "Nope. I thought we'd be fine." He glanced up at the sky. "The storm will be on you before I can get Susie or collect the Smithers. Don't worry. I'll keep an eye on them. You should go now and get these folks to safety."

"The building is new so you should be okay." The man peered up at the condominium blinking against the rain. "Secure yourselves the best you can. What are your names?" He took a small notepad from his pocket and scribbled down their names, then narrowed his gaze at him. "I'll make sure someone checks on you the moment the danger passes." The man climbed into the front of the bus and the doors shut behind him.

Branch dashed back inside, secured the doors then headed for the stairs. With each step, the building whined in complaint. Wind screamed through the shutters adding a locomotive's whistle to the oncoming storm. By the time he reached his floor, sweat coated his skin and dripped from the tip of his nose. Panting, he crunched through broken glass toward his apartment. The wind howled like a devil through the broken window and pummeled his back plastering his clothes with leaves and bits of garbage. A whip-like crack split through the roaring wind then glass shards broke from the shattered window frame and flew into the wall like ice daggers. *Holy shit!* He sidestepped the broken glass and dashed inside. "Susie, where are you?"

He moved swiftly into the kitchen, picked up the radio and the lantern then noticing the survival packs were missing headed toward the bedrooms. At least Susie had taken his advice. Pushing open the door, he lifted the lantern and finding the room empty turned to search the other rooms. Damn, he would have to secure one room the best he could and ride out the storm.

"I'm here under the bed." Susie's voice came out in a squeak.

"Thank God." Branch placed the lantern on the nightstand and bent to peer under the bedspread. "It's okay you can come out now." He offered her his hand. "Bring everything you need into my room. I'll stow your bags in the bathroom with mine, that's the safest place. We'll push the cupboards in front of the windows for extra protection." He reached for her bags, glad to see she had one of the survival kits hanging over one shoulder. "I'll get you settled and safe, then I'll get extra supplies from the kitchen just in case we get stuck."

"It's bad, isn't it?" Susie's face had drained of color. "I saw the window in the passageway blowout. Did you manage to help the old people downstairs?"

"Yeah, it's bad, but they refused to leave. They told me about another couple sheltering in the foyer. I went downstairs to help them and heard a horn. It was a bus picking up people for the

Evacuation Center, but I couldn't risk everyone's lives by asking them to wait for us. The bus driver will let the authorities know we're here, so we'll just have to make the best of it." He shrugged nonchalantly to appear as casual as possible. He wanted to shield his concerns for their safety from her terrified gaze. "Honestly, I'd rather be here than on a damn bus right about now. I hope they make it out okay."

He led her into the bedroom and with her help pushed the heavy cupboards in front of the balcony window. "We should be safe enough in here. I'll go and get the rest of the supplies from the kitchen."

"*Please,* don't leave me alone again. I think my heart is going to explode out through my chest." Susie gripped his arm. "Are we going to die?"

He slid one arm around her shoulders and pulled her close. She wasn't stupid and deserved the truth. The storm was worse than he had imagined. "I hope not, darlin', but if I only have a few hours left, I couldn't think of a better person to share my last breath with." He stroked her hair. "Come on, we need to hurry. We don't have much time."

With all items secured in Branch's wardrobe and the bathroom window boarded up, Susie glanced around the bedroom. She trembled and tried desperately to push down the rising panic. The roaring wind and splattering of hail refused to stop its onslaught "Are you sure we have enough food and water? What if the roof caves in and we can't get to the other supplies?"

"The authorities know we're here. These packs will last a few days at least, and when the storm misses us and heads back out to sea, I'm sure we'll be laughing at all this preparation." He gave her a slow sexy smile and headed to the door. "I have fixings in the refrigerator for sandwiches and a fruitcake. We might as well eat now before the food goes bad. I dropped most of the other perishables into the freezer when I heard the first hurricane warning. It will keep for a couple of days if we don't open the lid."

She followed him into the kitchen to raid the refrigerator and under the soft glow of the lantern, helped him carry everything into his bedroom. After setting up the provisions on a coffee table, she sat crossed legged opposite him and made a sandwich before he secured the food inside a cold chest. "You are very competent. Are you used to surviving in unusual conditions?"

"The weather here and in Texas can be volatile, so sure, I'm used to preparing for tornadoes and the like. With global warming, I guess it's only going to get worse." He shrugged. "Truth is I don't think I'll ever get used to the noise. The wind can do so much damage, and here by the sea, it's a double whammy." He took a large bite of his stuffed bread roll and chewed slowly.

You're filling me with confidence. A shiver crawled up her spine. He had not joked about the noise of the wind. Howling gusts rocked the building and rattled the shutters. Flashes of lightning followed by endless rolls of thunder shook the earth like bomb blasts. Oh yeah, everything was just peachy. Appetite gone, she stared at her sandwich and instead of eating chewed her nails. Her attempt to portray a strong independent woman had flown completely out the window. If Branch had not been sitting opposite she would probably be hiding under her bed or worse running in the direction of the Evacuation Center. *Where the hell is that place anyway?*

She desperately wanted to speak to her mother but had some idea of her "I told you so" response. Unfortunately, she had argued with her about her decision to leave the UK and as her mother put it, "take sides" with her estranged father. Apart from the odd phone call, he had not contacted her very much at all over the years. She had no recollection of living with him and doubted she would recognize him in the flesh.

"A penny for your thoughts?" Branch touched her cheek with the rough tip of one finger.

She reached for her sandwich, more in a reflex action than hunger. "Oh, nothing really. I was thinking about my mother. We didn't part on very good terms. She didn't want me to come here and be close to my father. He never paid a cent in maintenance all the time I was growing up. I feel a bit guilty not making things right with her before I left home." She sighed and took a bite. A full mouth was a good excuse not to reply to his questions.

"I guess, if your father didn't support her and you left to come here, your mom might have thought you'd taken sides." Branch opened a bottle of water and sipped then looked at her thoughtfully. "Only a coward abandons a child. It's obvious he isn't poor if he owns the building next door and is planning to settle in Hawaii. Maybe your mom thinks he should have stood up and acted like a man."

"Yes, I think she wanted me to stay with her but she has remarried, and it was becoming *difficult* living in the same house with them." She pushed a lock of hair behind one ear. "So, when Dad offered me this job, I jumped at it."

"Holy cow, was the new husband coming on to you?" Branch frowned and his knuckles whitened around the bottle of water.

The memory of her bedroom doorknob turning and seeing a man's outline in the doorway made her heart race with fear. She lifted her chin and stared at him. "He didn't touch me, but he made me uncomfortable." Shuddering, she grimaced. "The thought of coming home and interrupting them . . . I'm sure you understand. It was best I left."

"Yeah, I think you did the right thing." Branch rubbed his chin. "I guess your mom thought moving stateside was a little extreme."

Susie shrugged and looked away. The last thing she wanted to do during her last hours on Earth was discuss her mother's new twenty-five-year-old husband.

After finishing her meal in silence, she pushed their paper plates into the garbage bag and then leaned back against the wall suddenly exhausted. "What time is it?"

"Eight-thirty." Branch held up the small radio for her to read the digital readout. "I'll see if the Hurricane Watch has issued any more warnings." He turned the switch and the speakers crackled into life.

"*The storm front is expected to cross the coast in the next ten minutes. Winds reaching one hundred and twenty miles per hour are . . .*"

A flash of lightning forced bright beams through the gaps in the shutters and the transmission dissolved into a loud buzzing sound. "Damn." Branch turned off the radio and slid an appraising eye over her. "You're exhausted. I think you should at least try to get some rest. We'll need our strength if anything happens, and if you're worried I'll stay awake to keep watch." He stood and held out a hand. "I'll shut the door and slide the nightstand across the opening. I've covered the bathroom window, so you'll be safe if you need to use the toilet. At least for now we have running water." He offered his hand and then pulled her to her feet. "Don't worry. I'll keep you safe. The storm will rush on by before you know it, and we'll soon have our lives back to normal."

Emotion rolled over her. He had to be the kindest and most gentle person she had met in her life. Lifting her chin, she captured the one hundred percent male beauty of him in her mind's eye to lock inside and keep forever. She understood the moment the storm passed, they would go their separate ways, but for now, she had him all to herself and would make the most of his company. She smiled trying to control the trembling in her bottom lip. "Thank you but would it be okay if I stayed close to you?"

"Sure." He rubbed the back of his neck and looked at her thoughtfully. "It's getting hot in here, so if you have something thin to sleep in it would help." He cleared his throat. "Keep a pair of jeans handy and shoes not sandals. There's broken glass everywhere, and I don't want you cutting yourself if we need to leave in a hurry."

She chewed on her bottom lip. The thought of sliding into bed with Branch half-naked would not stop the fear of the hurricane, but it would sure help. "Okay." She headed for the bathroom.

Branch swallowed hard at the idea of having her pressed against him all night. Damn, he would not be able to turn off his sex drive completely, especially not snuggled up to a half-naked beautiful woman. He tried to think of anything else but the hours ahead and made the room as safe as possible then stripped the bed leaving only the bottom sheet. Sweat ran down his forehead. *It's too hot for her to sleep in here.* He stared at the bathroom door for long moments, trying to think of a solution then remembered an old battery-operated fan belonging to his father. He searched the top of the cupboard and when he found it let out a cheer. The emergency packs had plenty of batteries, and soon he had the fan on the nightstand blowing cool air over the bed. He stripped to his jocks then dragged a pair of jeans, socks, and a clean tee shirt from his chest of drawers, and added them to his boots under the bed. He made sure he had his wallet, phone, and flashlight within reach.

Worst-case scenario they would have to climb through debris to leave the building. High winds might do significant damage, but his apartment should withstand an earthquake. He would have to try to instill confidence in Susie but understood the danger, and it had taken a considerable amount of effort to push down his rising panic. *Stay cool, or she will go ballistic.* If she would allow him to cuddle her, it might soothe her nerves. She acted as if she liked him and trusted him to keep her safe. The idea sent a circle of warmth around his heart. He shook his head in disbelief, trying to grasp the fact he had only known her for one day. Her slightly eccentric manner made him relax and forget his crazy lifestyle existed. *It feels like I've known her for years.*

He moved around the apartment checking the windows and stowing any items that might cause injury if a window smashed and left them at the mercy of the storm. Outside the hurricane howled. With each flash of lightning, thunder struck with the roar of a dragon. Debris, hail, and rain pelted the trembling building without respite. As he strolled back inside the bedroom, the bathroom door flew open, and Susie ran into his arms. He kicked the door shut then led her to the bed and sitting down pulled her into his arms. "Hold on, darlin', it sounds like it's heading our way."

Rolling onto the sheets, he stroked her hair, and rubbed one hand up and down her back, realizing she wore nothing beneath the flimsy cotton nightgown. He bit back a groan, but when her hands slid around his neck and she pressed timid kisses to his chest, his primal urges roared. *Oh, Lord.* Unable to resist, he lifted her chin and took her lips. She opened for him, and he explored every inch of her soft wet mouth. Dang, she tasted so good, and when her peppermint flavored tongue tangled with his, he wanted to devour every inch of her. He ran one hand up her silky thigh, under the edge of her nightgown and over her tiny strip of silk panties to explore her rounded buttocks. When she arched her back pushing her hard nipples against his chest, demanding attention, the fear of the hurricane and common sense fled. He inched the cotton fabric up her chest to expose her full, delicious breasts.

Without breaking the kiss, he cupped one full globe, weighed it in his hand then plucked at the taught hard bud. She moaned into his mouth and slipped one silky leg up his thigh opening her core to him. *Sweet Jesus.* Her feminine arousal filled his nose obliterating his common sense, and he hardened so fast his vision blurred. Dragging his mouth away from her tempting lips, he pressed kisses down her neck then closed his mouth over one delicious hard nipple. He tormented the bud flicking his tongue then nipping gently with his teeth.

"Oh, that feels so good." Susie raked his back and thrust her rounded hips forward. "Make love to me, Branch. I need you to make me forget the storm."

He lifted his head and stared into eyes filled with lust. He shook his head trying to control his raging desire. Oh yeah, he wanted her, and she was ready, willing, and able, but common sense reared its head. Not wanting or expecting a sexual encounter the last thing he had taken to bed was protection. He rolled away from her and seized his wallet. Plucking out a square packet, he sighed with relief. Most women practiced birth control, and she sure looked clean, but he did not take chances. He cleared his throat to bring her attention to him. "Are you sure, darlin', we only just met?"

"Sure?" Susie blinked at him as if trying to comprehend his question, then as if understanding, nodded. "Yes, I'm sure. Are you?"

He heaved a sigh of relief. "Hell, yeah."

Susie clung to him as his kisses and the exquisite way he suckled her breasts drove her crazy with desire. The storm raged, but his touch blocked out the fear. If fate had decided to take her life, she refused to die a bloody virgin. In fact, she could not think of a better way to spend her last night. When he kissed a path down her chest, circled her navel then slipped his hand between her thighs to explore her hairless mound all thoughts of hurricanes, or anything else fled. She had read erotic novels and fantasized alone in her bed at night, but nothing came close to the real thing. He caressed her, kissed down her torso then stroked her inner thighs with his rough fingertips, and she opened her legs for him. When his inquisitive tongue slipped between her folds, she cried out in ecstasy tossing her head delirious with erotic desire. Her muscles trembled with every swirl of his tongue around her sensitive spot. Oh, man, he was so good at lovemaking. Hoping he would not stop, she sank her hands into his thick, black hair and held on.

A myriad of wonderful sensations surged along every nerve ending sending flames of lust deep inside her. Wonderful spirals of heat curled in her belly and she lifted her hips in an effort to receive more of his delicious attention. He held her firmly with his strong hands and lapped relentlessly. Lost in a world of erotic euphoria, she let go of his hair and gripped the sheets. "Oh God, I can't take so much pleasure. I'm going to explode."

"That's the idea, darlin'." He chuckled deep, feral, and lifted his head then blew on her oversensitive nub. "Mmm, you taste so good, and I'm not going to rush. I like my lovin' slow, and I want to feel you tremble against my lips." His head bent, and he closed his hot mouth over her throbbing center and sucked.

A swell of incredible delight surged over her in a huge wave, and with muscles twitching, an orgasm hit her with such ferocity she let out a sob. "*Branch.* Oh, my God."

Laying between her thighs, Branch kissed his way back up her damp body, nibbled each hard nipple then crushed her mouth in a long possessive kiss. He ached to be deep inside her but wanted to be sure that she realized what she was doing. She seemed so innocent in his arms, and her tentative movements made him cautious. He tore open the condom and noticed the way she averted her eyes. Darn, most of his lovers insisted taking charge and used their mouth to do the honors. "Do you want me inside you, darlin'? Is it okay for me to keep going?"

"Yes." Her gaze moved over his face. "*Please.*"

When she lifted her knees and wrapped her legs around his waist, he moaned his approval and suited up. He slid against her slick entrance. Lord, she was so darn wet. With a roll of his hips, he slid a few inches inside, but when her nails dug into his shoulders, he paused waiting for her to change her mind. He had not had sex with a woman who was so small and tight. She had mentioned not having many boyfriends, so it might have been a while since her last lover. With effort, he forced back the need to plunge deep and take her hard and fast. He watched her face half shadowed in the lamplight and eased inside with gentle care. Her eyes rounded and small white teeth bit her bottom lip. He froze in mid-slide. "Are you okay?"

"Yes, but you're bigger than I expected." She winced at a loud crash of thunder and tightened her grip.

He smiled with masculine satisfaction. Most women appreciated his larger than average size, and he made damn sure they were slick and ready for him. He would soon make her forget the storm. "More to please you, ma'am. Just relax, and I'll take it nice and slow." The moment her muscles softened around him, he slid in to the hilt then kissed her long and slow waiting for her to adjust to his bulk. Inhaling the scent of lavender soap and woman, he lifted his head. "Better?"

"Mmm." She closed her eyes and the corners of her mouth curled into a smile.

He started slowly, rocking his hips trying to ease the tight grip she had around his shaft. She fitted him so well, and with each thrust, her little moans of delight pushed him closer to the edge. *Slow down and make it good for her.* He pulled out and rolled her onto her knees. Apart from giving him a confused expression, she complied. He circled her clit from behind until she moaned in approval and rubbed against him. "That's it, darlin', push up for me. Dang, you are so hot and wet."

Taking hold of her hips, he thrust deep. She closed around him like a warm glove. When she moaned and panted, he rode her hard allowing his climax 'free rein. Against his thighs her legs trembled, her tight channel clenched around him pulsating, and she cried out. He needed more and swirled his hips pounding her until heat curled around his groin and rushed to his tip. Pushing deep, he fell into orgasmic delight, and as he spilled, the danger of the storm faded into the void.

He awoke hearing a loud whine followed by a ripping sound and glanced at the clock on the nightstand. Holy cow, they had been asleep for four hours or more. Under him, Susie gasped and wriggled to get free. He rolled to one side and touched her shoulder. "It's okay, calm down."

"It's *not* okay. It sounds like the hurricane is tearing off the roof." She rolled over to face him. "It's getting worse, I'm sure."

Wanting to reassure her, he pressed a kiss to her damp cheek. "I'm pretty sure we're entering the eye of the storm. It will be quiet for a while then get bad again. This is the edge of the first wave. That noise is probably the wind tossing around tin roofs or garden sheds, and they're hitting the building. If water starts running down the walls, we'll know something's wrong." He stroked her cheek and emotion rolled over him. "It will be over soon, I promise." Brushing a kiss over her moist lips, he sighed. "If it hangs around I think I'd enjoy holding you in my arms all night."

A loud crash and the sound of glass breaking came from the sitting room, and the bedroom door rattled. Susie sat bolt upright pulling down her nightgown.

"Oh, my God, something smashed through the shutters."

He let out a long sigh. *Man, this lady is skittish.* "Like I said, it *will* settle down soon as the eye of the storm passes over us. Then it could get bad again. It depends if it's changed direction or not but I have a feeling it's not over yet." He slid one arm around her shoulders in an attempt to calm her. "Listen, the wind has dropped already."

"So, we have at least a few minutes to move around in safety?" She scrambled from the bed and dashed into the bathroom then turned in the doorway to look at him. "Come on, we should put on some clothes before we take a look outside."

"It's safer to stay in here." He patted the bed. "The windows are covered. Come back to bed and snuggle with me."

"Oh, I would *really* like that, truly I would." Susie blushed to the tips of her ears. "That" — she waved one hand shyly toward the rumpled bedsheets — "was wonderful, but if I can't look outside and you think it's safe, I would like to have a wash. I'm sure you understand?"

He leaned up on one elbow and smiled at her. She looked so beautiful in the lamplight all tousled and sexy. "You'll be fine. If the water isn't running we have plenty of bottles but don't bother getting dressed, it's too hot in here, and we aren't going anywhere."

"Thank you, but I think I'll pull on a pair of panties." Susie gave him a wide smile. "When the storm is over, I would like to check if my building is still standing and I'm not running down the street half-naked. What would happen if I slipped and fell or got hit by flying debris and needed to be rescued?" She giggled, and the sound was like tiny bells. "Can you imagine what my father would say if I made the news bare-assed over a fireman's back?"

He tried unsuccessfully to block the image from his mind and laughed. Rubbing his chin, he let his gaze move over her. "Don't worry. I'll look after you, darlin'."

"Maybe now, but I'll have to stand on my own two feet once this is over. I'm responsible for my father's building, and I have a feeling I'll be putting in insurance claims for weeks and so will you." She rubbed her arms and stared at the bedroom door. "I wish I could go outside and see what's happening."

His stomach dropped in a deep feeling of loss. With her, it had not been casual sex. The earth had moved with Susie. *Is this what it feels like when I leave a girl after a one-night stand?* He once refused to admit he used the women he had loved and left as all the women's magazines professed, but realization slammed into him. Damn! Susie had turned the tables on him by refusing to return to his bed. Usually, women begged *him* to stay, and Susie sure as hell had not given him the impression she had enjoyed what he had imagined to be incredible sex. Deciding to try harder next time if he got the chance, he raised up on one elbow. "It's dangerous out there and dark without streetlights. There will be debris everywhere and broken glass." As if God had sent a sign, the building shuddered against a gust of roaring wind. He offered her his best sexy smile. "See, it's nowhere near over. Go take a wash then come back to bed, darlin'."

"Okay, I'll be a few minutes. If there's water, I really need to take a shower." She peeked around the door and smiled so cutely his stomach flipped. "Mind if I leave the door open and move the light a little closer? It's dark in there."

Scared like a rabbit and now she wants to take a shower. He wished she had invited him to join her and sighed in disappointment. "Go right ahead, but the water might be off so take a few bottles with you as well, just in case."

Moments later, he could hear water running in the shower, and a puff of steam leaked out the door. *At least the gas hot water system is working.* When a roll of thunder shook the windows, Susie let out a cry, and he wanted to run to her side. "Are you okay?"

"Y–yes. I just have to convince myself it's safe in here."

Branch squashed the surge of lust at the image of her naked and wet. "I'm right here if you need me."

He rubbed his chin and inhaled. Oh, man, he could smell her sweet feminine fragrance on his fingers, and his length filled eager for more. Hell, he'd been around the block many times, yet she had made him lose control, and he wanted more of her. Not just her body, he *really* liked her company. Susie was a special girl, nice, sweet, and treated him like a normal guy. He ground his back teeth in frustration. Once the hurricane passed, she would no longer need his protection and would walk out of his life. He wanted to get to know her, perhaps fall in love. He slapped a palm against his forehead. To think he would actually consider giving up his fiercely protected bachelorhood hours after meeting Susie, but he had to admit she was an amazingly special woman. *I must be losing my mind.*

CHAPTER FOUR

Susie's wail of fear echoed in the small room and unable to contain his concern a moment longer, Branch slipped from the bed and headed toward the bathroom. "Need company, darlin'?" He moved inside the dim room. "It's awful dark in there, and I don't like you being afraid. Do you want me to bring the light?"

"Could you?" Susie peered around the shower door. "I can't find the soap."

"I'm sure I can help." Branch strolled into the bedroom and grabbed the lantern. He took a bottle of shower gel from the shelf and handed it to her. "Anything else you need?"

"Only *you.*" Susie stared at him from beneath dripping hair her eyes wide and scared. "I feel safer when you're close. The storm is getting worse again, and it sounds like the roof may go at any moment. Would you mind very much taking a shower with me?"

Oh, darlin', don't say that, I am just a man, and you are tempting me beyond reason. Hoping the dim light would hide his growing erection, he smiled. "Sure, but we'll need to hurry. Soon as we're done here, I'll turn on the radio see if I can find an update on the storm." He slipped naked behind her and taking the gel from her, lathered his hands, and biting the inside of his cheek to quell his raging desire, ran the suds over her smooth flesh. "There is that better?"

"Uh-huh. Mmm, you do that so well." Susie glanced over one shoulder at him. "Have you ever thought of becoming a masseuse? I bet women would line up around the block to have you relieve their tension."

He snorted. "Well, ma'am, I couldn't think of a better occupation, but I'd need the stamina of a bull to keep them all happy." He ran the suds down her arms. "But you, I could manage." He nipped her earlobe.

When she leaned back into his embrace, the urgency of the storm vanished in a wave of lust. Thunder crashed, and Susie stiffened beneath his palms. "We'd better rinse off and get dressed pronto. It sounds like the hurricane is going to give us another thrill ride before it's over."

Susie gripped the waistband of her jeans with trembling fingers and hopped on one leg in an effort to push the other inside. The flashes of lightning had become intense, and the following rolls of thunder came fast on their heels and sounded like bombs dropping. The building shook rattling the shutters, and the accompanying whine did nothing to ensure her confidence. She reached for a tee shirt and pulled it over her white cotton bra then turned to look at Branch. He had dressed swiftly and was checking the crackling broadcast on the radio for any news of the storm. Moving toward the bed, she peered around for her shoes and socks. She sat down to feel around the floor and found her leather ankle boots tucked under the bed. Slipping them on, she flinched at each flash of lightning. The howling storm had increased in intensity and by the amount of debris, hitting the building had gained strength in the last hour. Beside her, Branch fiddled with the knobs on the radio trying to find a station giving out information, but the interference from the storm was the only sound issuing from the tiny speakers.

He turned to her, and for the first time since they had sheltered from the hurricane, his expression was one of concern.

"I can't get any news. In fact, I can't find a station broadcasting." Branch pushed a hand through his dark hair and set the radio on the table beside the bed. He took a deep breath and let it whistle out between his teeth. "It's probably because the cloud cover is dense at the moment. I'll try again later. Don't worry, we'll be fine." He pushed to his feet with a sigh and glanced around the room. "Are you hungry? I have coffee in the thermos bottle and fruitcake." He rubbed his stomach. "I'm famished."

She let her gaze move slowly up to his face, even afraid of the storm she could appreciate the handsome man standing before her. Oh boy, add great lover to his list of pros, and she had hit the jackpot. She smiled up at him. "Yes, that would be lovely, thank you."

After finishing the coffee and the fruitcake, Susie tried desperately to put the sound of the raging hurricane to the back of her mind. She would be useless if she had to deal with an emergency. Panic had become the enemy and Branch's sudden change of demeanor worried her. She touched his arm to get his attention away from staring at the trickle of water running from the wall beside the window. "That's not good, is it?"

"I'll put towels down to soak up the water before it ruins the carpet." Branch gave her an encouraging smile. "I'd say the glass is broken and the rain is blowing in. I'm not going to risk moving the wardrobe from in front of the window to check the damage." He heaved a long sigh. "It may be safer if we move everything into the bathroom. It is the safest place to be in a hurricane, unless of course, we had a root cellar." He grinned. "Personally, I wouldn't have one on the beachfront. With my luck, it would probably fill with water." He bent to pick up the survival packs and a case of bottled water. "Take everything from the bed and pile it into the bathtub."

Susie collected bed linen and pillows. She dashed into the bathroom to drop them in the tub then returned for her small bag and glanced at him. "We'll need to pack a few changes of clothes, in case we have to leave in a hurry."

"Okay and make sure you have ID in the pocket of your jeans." He moved toward the dresser collected a few items of clothing then stuffed them in one of the backpacks hanging from a peg on the back of the door. After dropping the bag at his feet, he took the second one and handed it to her. "Put your things in here. It's waterproof, and if we have to leave, you'll need something easy to carry."

"Okay." She quickly complied then dropped the bag inside the bathroom door.

Before she could take the next breath, a loud ripping sound cut through the air obliterating the sound of the storm. The next moment the plaster on the walls popped and crumbled. A gaping crack opened in the wall. Susie stared at it uncomprehending for a few seconds before Branch took her arm and pushed her into the bathroom. The backpacks followed along with the cooler containing food and her suitcase. He snatched up his hat then followed close behind his mouth set in a grim line.

"Get into the tub." He climbed in behind her and pulled the quilt over their heads.

When Branch pulled her against his hard chest and wrapped his arms and legs around her, she held on tight. All hell broke loose around them with the fury of a raging bull. She cried out in terror, but Branch held her cheek hard against his chest mumbling comforting words in her ear. The bathroom door crashed open, and a vicious, destructive wind rocked the small room tearing at the blinds and tossing toiletries from the shelves. As glass shattered peppering them with shards, she silently thanked God for Branch's quick thinking. The thick quilt may have protected them from injury but not from flying debris. When something thumped into them, Branch let out a moan, and a shudder went through his chest. She looked up at him and ran a hand over his back. "Are you hurt? I can't feel any blood."

"I'll do." Branch rolled his shoulders. "Something hit me in the back. Probably the bottle of aftershave I left it on the shelf. I should have removed anything that could have caused injury." He gave her a gentle squeeze. "We should be through the worst of it soon."

Soon, what a joke. She clung to him and for what seemed like hours of riding every horrific ride at an amusement park. Then as quickly as the storm had started the wind died down and a strange, eerie calm fell over the apartment. "Is it over?"

"Yeah, I think so." Branch gingerly lifted the corner of the quilt sending a shower of glass tinkling to the tile. "Cover your eyes for a moment until I'm sure it's safe."

Pulling the neck of her tee shirt up over her face, she pressed both hands over her eyes and waited in trepidation. After some time, Branch touched her shoulder. She peeked out of the top of her shirt and gaped at the damage. One side of the bedroom wall was in ruins, rubble, leaves and tree branches littered the bedroom floor. Rain fell through the hole, and a river of water ran across the bedroom floor and pooled around the bathtub. "Oh, my God!"

"You can say that again." Branch ran a hand down his face then turned his attention back to her. "Stay here, I'm going to see how much damage the building sustained on the other side. I hope we can get out via the fire escape."

"No!" Susie jumped to her feet. "I'm not staying here on my own. We might have one chance to get out before the entire building comes down on us." She stepped onto the broken glass glad she had the foresight to wear boots. "Grab the bags and let's get the hell out of here."

Branch brushed the glass fragments from the backpacks then handed one to Susie. He slammed on his black Stetson then added a few more bottles of water to each bag. "I've packed a pile of sleeping bags, extra supplies, fuel, and a guitar in the boot of my Mustang just in case something happened. If I can gain access to the parking lot, I'll go and collect them. The car will be useless if the roads are blocked with rubble but I do have a motorcycle." Holding out his hand. He offered her his best confident smile, but inside the realization they had reached an untenable position, cramped his guts. The chances of getting out the building alive had to be less than ten percent looking at the damage. "Come on then, darlin', pick up your survival kit and stick to me like glue." He snatched up his supplies and held out his free hand to her.

"Don't worry I've just become your Siamese twin." Susie's warm hand wrapped around his fingers. "Go slow my legs don't seem to be working very well. I think I'm still in panic mode." She had her backpack on her shoulders and collected her survival bag before taking his hand.

He turned and grinned at her. "You got it, darlin'."

Leading the way around the rubble, he slowly moved toward the gaping hole that used to be the front door of his apartment. In the hallway, the storm had strewn glass from one end to the other. Twisted aluminum window frames and rubbish had piled up in front of the fire door leading to the stairs. "Don't move from this spot. Here take my bag."

He took a large tree branch and gouged a path to the exit then led Susie into the stairwell. He breathed a sigh of relief, ahead the stairs were free of debris. "We're in luck as long as the next three flights are undamaged." As he took his bag, his thoughts went to the old couple living downstairs. "I hope the Smithers are okay. Their apartment is on this side of the building, so maybe they missed out on the damage."

"I hope so too." Susie gripped his hand tightly. "They seem a very nice couple."

Certain he could hear voices Branch paused on the stairs. "Listen, can you hear someone speaking?"

They stood in silence for some moments before Susie smiled at him.

"Yes, it sounds more like a conversation than someone calling out for help."

"It sure does." He moved down the stairs glad that Susie followed close behind without stumbling. Her legs seem to be working fine now.

As they reached the Smithers floor, Branch could see the old couple sitting on the steps. "Hey, are you both okay?"

"Yes, I think the fire escape is the only area that escaped damage." Mr. Smithers helped his wife to her feet. "We need to get outside before the whole damn building comes down on us."

Branch turned to Susie. "Will you be okay?"

"Yes, it looks safe enough in here." Susie smiled at him and her cheeks pinked.

He held out his free arm to Mrs. Smithers. "May I help you, ma'am?"

"You are such a gentleman." The old lady smiled at him and took his arm.

"I'll go first." Mr. Smithers moved down the stairs with Susie close behind.

Branch followed behind them supporting Mrs. Smithers. "My main concern is where we go from here."

"I've lived through quite a few hurricanes, and they are selective. Sometimes they wipe out an entire neighborhood, other times they pick and choose which building they're going to destroy. If everything is flattened, we'll have to hope we can make it to the nearest shelter." Mr. Smithers turned to look at him. "If not, it shouldn't take too long before help arrives. Last time we waited in the amenities block for six days before they found us. At least, the authorities know where we are and will come looking for us eventually."

"If we are isolated don't forget, I have my motorcycle, so unless it's flooded" — Branch grimaced at the notion of his vintage Indian, ruined by seawater — "I might be able to go for help."

"Can you make that *we* can go for help?" Susie stumbled down the stairs behind him and crashed into his back. "Sorry, my legs keep shaking. I think I'm still worried about the storm."

He stopped on the landing and turned to her smiling. He had so many perfect women in his life, her clumsiness made her as cute as a button. "Didn't I tell you, I'd look after you?" He released Mrs. Smithers's arm to cup Susie's cheek. "I'm not leaving you anywhere alone. Cross my heart and hope to die." He pushed down the need to drag her into his arms and kiss the worry from her eyes. "Come on now, only one flight of stairs to go then we can see what the damage is outside."

"I'll be fine. You help Mrs. Smithers." Susie gripped the handrail with trembling fingers and her mouth quivered in an attempt at a smile.

"Okay." Reluctantly he took Mrs. Smithers by the elbow and proceeded down the steps at a snail's pace. He would have to make sure the old couple would be secure in a safe place to wait for assistance. With luck, the rescue team would already be on its way. He bit back a groan at the sight of the dirty water covering the floor in front of the fire door and turned to the group. "Wait here, I'll see if I can open the door." He handed his bags to Susie then moved down the steps to depress the bar across the fire exit.

The door moved a few inches, and muddy water seeped inside the building. Pressing one shoulder against the door, he drew a deep breath and pushed, but the door only opened a crack. Something had blocked the exit and trapped them. He tried again, his boots slipping in the water pooling under the door. "It's stuck."

The next moment Susie was beside him her face flushed.

"If we push together I might be able to see what's stopping it moving." She moved beside him and wedged one shoulder against the door.

He smiled down at her. "You push down on the handle, darlin', and I'll shoulder charge the door. On the count of three. One, two, three."

The door made a grinding sound then swung half-open. Wet sand slid into the hallway and rush of cool salty wind blasted his face. He stepped cautiously outside then swallowed hard. Dear Lord have mercy, the entire row of beachfront condominiums were nothing more than piles of kindling and twisted metal. Worried about distressing the others, he held up his hand to prevent them following him. Three pairs of wide eyes stared at him expectantly. His chest tightened. In a few seconds, they would discover the magnitude of the disaster awaiting them all. Apart from being homeless, the looters and sightseers would crawl out of the woodwork to prey on the survivors. *Funny how they manage to arrive before FEMA.* He rolled his shoulders determined to protect his little group from harm, although Susie would be shocked if she knew he carried a Glock in his backpack. *Better safe than sorry.* "Wait here, and I'll check if it's safe to leave." He cleared his throat. "Prepare yourselves for a shock. It's real bad out there."

The storm had gutted the houses and picked clean their remains. The once pristine buildings resembled a pile of bare bones in the desert. Rubble, sand, palm trees, and an untouched window box containing yellow daisies had come to rest against the remaining wall of the coffee shop where hours before he had spent time with Susie. A red sofa sat under burst pipe gushing out water ten feet tall to create an absurdly beautiful fountain. *It's like Armageddon out there.* Turning, he stared up at the tattered remains of his building. The structural damage was considerate, and they had been fortunate to escape with their lives. Luckily, the underbuilding parking lot entrance remained untouched, but there would be no escape by car. The roads had blended into a trash dump landscape as if they had not existed. Heart racing with shock, he moved his attention down the road to the amenities block and sighed with relief. Although covered with debris the small cinder brick building appeared to be intact and would be a safe haven for now. He turned to Mr. Smithers. "It looks like the amenities building hasn't suffered much damage, but I can't say the same for the rest of the beachfront. We'll have to be very careful crossing the road because there's a mess of broken glass and rubble everywhere."

"We've survived hurricanes many a time." Mrs. Smithers gripped her husband's arm. "Although I'm thinking of moving inland now. I think our luck is close to running out."

"Is my building damaged?" Susie hesitated on the bottom step, her eyes wide with fear.

Branch moved to her side and placed one arm around her shoulders. "I'm afraid it's gone, and this one is uninhabitable. We'll need to find shelter, and right now, the shower block across the road is our best option.

"Do you know if the owners of the coffee shop got out in time?" Susie gripped his arm.

He shook his head. "I'm not sure but they were packing up when we left, so I guess so."

A loud creaking sound broke through the eerie silence. "Watch out!" He jumped back to avoid a large piece of concrete plummeting from above and hitting the wet ground with a loud *thwack*. "We have to leave right now. Come on." He collected his bags and ushered everyone out the door. "Get across the road and into the open before this building falls down. Hurry."

With Mr. Smithers determined to help his wife, Branch dragged in a deep breath and turned to face Susie. She had frozen at the exit with a white-knuckle grip on her bag. He moved toward her and touched her on the shoulder. "Come here, darlin'." Hell, the poor girl was shaking all over. He drew her under his free arm then dropped his voice into a low, soothing tone. "Best you look straight ahead toward the beach. When you have time to catch your breath, you can look at the damage."

She flashed him a glance of pure desperation.

"What are we going to do?"

Taking it slow, he guided her out into the misty rain and headed toward the shower block. "In situations like this one, we'll have to wait until FEMA gets organized and comes to rescue us."

"FEMA?" Susie trudged beside him her step hesitant and slow. "Who is that?"

He urged her onward carefully avoiding the bricks and other rubbish covering the sandy road. In fact, the street looked more like a creek bed than the usual blacktop shimmering in the heat.

He gave her a squeeze. "FEMA is the Emergency Management Agency. They'll come but will take time. I have no idea how far this damage extends or if other places have been affected." He sighed with relief the moment they arrived at the amenities building. "I have the radio in my bag, and as soon as we're settled, I'll see if there's any news." He smiled at her upturned face. "I doubt the cell phones will work, but we can give them a try." He pulled out his phone and stared at the screen. "Nah, no signal."

"What about the things in your car and your motorcycle?" Susie stepped onto the littered sidewalk and turned to look up at the wrecked buildings. "The entry to the parking lot looks pretty clear. Do you think we should try and at least get the motorcycle before the building collapses?" She covered her mouth with trembling fingers.

Branch shot a glance over one shoulder wincing at the sight of his building. "First, we make sure the shower block is safe and get settled. Once the wind dies down and it stops raining, then I'll see if it's safe to go into the parking lot." He wanted to reassure her but going under his building would be as dangerous as riding a wild bull with a red-hot poker shoved up its ass.

CHAPTER FIVE

Susie scanned the area in disbelief. Nothing Branch could have said would have prepared her for the devastation. She gripped his arm, and her pulse pounded in her ears as she moved her attention slowly along the destroyed beachfront properties. The wind had dropped, and an eerie silence surrounded them. The waves pounded on the beach as usual, but the call of seagulls had ceased as if everything on the planet had died leaving them alone. Could there be survivors trapped inside the piles of rubble? She glanced back at Branch and pushed words past the lump in her throat. "I think we need to look for survivors."

"Yes, we do, but first we'll need to make sure the Smithers are safe, and then we'll worry about everybody else." Branch led her toward the shower block. "I doubt very much many people remained behind to ride out the storm. Most people who live in this area are fully aware of the danger."

Susie pushed the horrific images of dead bodies from her mind and followed Mr. and Mrs. Smithers into the amenities block. Divided into men and women's facilities, the building was big enough to give both couples privacy.

"We'll take the men's showers." Mr. Smithers indicated to the sand-encrusted doorway. "It will be easy enough to make ourselves a comfortable bed inside one of the shower stalls. We can lock the door overnight just in case we have any unwanted guests." He led his wife to the other side of the building, and they disappeared inside.

"He has a point." Branch tipped back his hat and looked down at her. "Do you mind sharing a shower stall with me? I know we don't have anything to sleep on at the moment, but it should be safe enough to go into the parking lot, and if I can get my car without a problem, I'll go back for my motorcycle."

She wanted to yell "Don't leave me" but bit back the words. The thought of him leaving her even for a few minutes in this barren wasteland scared the hell out of her. "I want to go with you." She met his stern gaze. "I'm afraid of being left alone" — she waved a hand toward the damaged building — "and you can't possibly risk going in there without me."

"I can and I will." Branch took a step back, and a nerve twitched in his cheek as if she had annoyed him. "I know you're frightened, hey, that's normal after going through such a terrifying experience, but I need you to make sure the old couple is okay. It was one hell of a shock for them too, and a few soothing words from you would go a long way." He gave her a smile, which did not reach his eyes then squeezed her shoulder. "Take our bags inside, and I'll be back before you I know I'm missing. When I drive out, I don't want to see you waiting here for me and worrying — understand? Your job is to make the shower block inhabitable." Bending, he brushed a kiss over her lips, and his expression softened. "Don't be concerned about me, darlin', I'll be fine. I broke the sprint track record at college, and if all hell breaks loose, I'll be out of there quick smart." He shoved his hat down firmly on his head then strode toward the parking lot without a backward glance.

She swallowed hard and fought the need to run after him. *I can do this.* She picked up Branch's bags and moved inside the amenities block then stowed the bags on the bench inside the first dry shower stall. She needed to keep busy and stop worrying about him. He would appreciate coming back to a comfortable place to stay. She glanced at the sand and leaves littering the floor then moved her attention to a locked cupboard set in the wall. No doubt, behind the door was storage for cleaning utensils and supplies. If she could open the door, perhaps there would be a broom inside to sweep the floor. Remembering the small toolkit Branch had pushed inside his backpack, she went back to the cubicle, crouched down, and unzipped the pockets one by one.

The sight of a pistol inside a leather holster made her blood run cold. She jumped back, slipped in the wet sand and sprawled on the floor legs thrashing to get away.

"Are you okay, my dear?" Mrs. Smithers appeared at the entrance her face pale and drawn.

I am such an idiot. "Yes, I tripped, but I'm fine, thank you." Susie pushed to her feet and brushed the sand from her jeans.

"You don't look well." Mrs. Smithers patted her arm. "Is there anything I can do to help?"

Grateful for the understanding, she smiled at her. "Thank you, but I'm okay. Although, I expect I'll be a little on edge for some time. I've haven't experienced a storm like that before."

"It's a fact of life living here." Mrs. Smithers glanced around then frowned. "I was looking for Branch. Has he gone for help?"

Facing her fear of weapons, Susie moved in front of the backpack. "No, he went into the parking lot to get his car." She did not want Mrs. Smithers to notice the gun sticking out of the bag's open pocket and walked her outside into the sunshine. Shaken, she forced her lips into a smile. "There are sleeping bags and supplies in the trunk. I wanted to go with him, but he insisted on going alone." She frowned and stared in the direction of the parking lot. "That building doesn't look safe. I hope he can retrieve the car before it collapses."

"Here he comes now." Mrs. Smithers gripped her arm. "Men! They act like children sometimes. Surely he knows revving the car like that will bring the building down on top of him."

A powerful engine's roar broke the silence, and a red Mustang launched out of the dark entrance. At the wheel, Branch skidded the powerful vehicle around the obstacles in the road, sending up a shower of wet sand before mounting the sidewalk and sliding to a stop in front of the amenities block. Without saying a word, he slipped from the car and leaving the door open, took off at a run toward the parking lot then disappeared into the building. Susie gaped in horror as deep cracks appeared in the wall and large clumps of cement rained down onto the footpath. She cried out in fear then covered her mouth, her attention riveted on the entrance.

"Dear Lord it's coming down." Mrs. Smithers gripped Susie's arm and dragged her back toward the toilet block. "Why did he go back inside?"

Numb with fear for Branch's safety, she prayed silently, hoping the building would hold for a few precious minutes. Aware of the woman's tight grip on her arm, she took a deep breath. "He wanted to get his motorcycle."

"Did Branch go back to the condo?" Mr. Smithers moved to his wife's side. "Damn fool."

The building creaked and groaned showering the road with debris. Minutes dragged by then she heard the distant sound of the cranking of motorcycle's engine. Branch tried many times before it burst into life then to her relief a motorcycle shot up the ramp into the open, chrome gleaming in the sunshine and headed toward them, weaving in and out of the garbage littering the road. Behind him, the building moaned its final goodbye and collapsed like a house of cards. A huge mushroom of dust rose into the air and Susie followed Mr. and Mrs. Smithers inside the amenities block. As they hovered at the entrance, she moved past them, grasped Branch's backpack, and dropped it gently back inside the dry cubicle, then closed the door.

The rumble of the motorcycle's engine filled the room, and she turned to see Branch grinning at her through a mask of white powder.

"It must be my lucky day." He slid from the bike, then pushed it almost reverently into a shower stall and closed the door. "Although my hat needs a clean." He removed his Stetson and swiped it against his thigh sending up great clouds of dust then pushed it back on his head.

Anger for risking his life welled up mixed with relief at seeing him safe. "If what has happened to you today is considered *lucky* I would hate to see you in a bad week."

"Oh darlin', I met you, and I saved my Indian." Branch chuckled and pushed his Stetson off his face. "And we're all alive."

They huddled together inside the shower block for some time before Branch glanced toward the entrance. "I think it's safe to go out now. He turned to Mr. Smithers and raised one eyebrow. "What's it like on your side of the building?"

"Much the same as here." Mr. Smithers followed them out the door. "There is a couple of dry spots we can use."

Moving through the doorway, Susie stopped mid-stride and gaped at her surroundings. Papers and strips of aluminum foil hung from what trees remained like old Christmas decorations. A white film covered everything as far as she could see. As if in the few minutes they had been inside, snow had covered the beachfront coating the skeletal ruins. Her gaze moved to the red Mustang. Only the side facing the amenities block displayed the pristine paint job. The rest of the car wore a cloak of dust and debris, but to her surprise, Branch did not appear distressed by the damage. He strolled to the back of the car and opened the trunk with his keys then gave her a brilliant smile.

She stared at him in disbelief. They were homeless and had lost everything. "I guess from your positive attitude you've been in this situation before?"

"Nope but now we have transport it will be easier to find help." Branch slipped an arm around her waist and pulled her against him. "The evacuation shelter is about ten miles inland, but first I'm taking a ride around the immediate area in case there are people needing assistance. Although, it looks quiet and I haven't noticed anyone wandering the streets. While I'm away, I want you to listen to the radio for any news."

"I can listen to the radio, and we can sort out the supplies." Mrs. Smithers patted him on the arm. "Best you keep the young lady with you. I don't think she is coping very well at the moment."

"That sounds like a plan. Thank you kindly, ma'am. Keep trying for a cell phone signal as well and if you can get through to the authorities let them know our position." Branch turned to Susie. "We'll do a sweep of the area." He removed his Stetson and ambled to the car then after tossing his hat inside took two helmets from the dust-covered trunk. He strolled back to his motorcycle and handed a helmet to Susie. "Put this on, we don't know what might be flying around out there." He pulled on his helmet then turned toward the shower block. "Just give me a minute. I'm starving."

A few moments later, he returned, with a wide grin and handful of energy bars. He slid onto the seat of his motorcycle then motioned her to follow.

Susie moved to his motorcycle and climbed on behind him. "Go slow."

"Put your arms around me, darlin'." Branch pulled her hands around his waist, and she hooked her fingers into his belt. He kicked the engine into life and raised his voice. "We'll head inland and see if there's a way through to the Evacuation Center."

Branch had used the pretense of collecting some energy bars from his survival pack to collect his Glock and shoulder holster. Although, no doubt Susie would be horrified, he had no idea who they would meet and disasters attracted the rats of society. He drove the Indian with care through the maze of rubbish stopping every so often to examine the skeletal remains of the once proud beachfront buildings for any signs of life. The rumble of the motorcycle's engine echoed against the few remaining walls in an eerie reminder of scenes from an apocalyptic movie. As they turned up the remains of a street, a wave of anxiety hit him and his pulse raced. Could they be the only people left alive? He killed the engine and glanced around to get his bearings, but the once familiar roads all appeared the same. The landmarks had vanished and before him lay destruction for as far as the eye could see.

The stench of raw sewage accosted his nose and ahead, a tree with its limbs devoid of leaves wore an assortment of clothes hanging from shattered branches. Rubbing his chin, he viewed the area in dismay. The children's toys and the huge amount of shoes scattered around made the horror so damn real. He turned at a rustling sound to see tumbleweed balls of paper rolling lazily past. In the middle of a twisted pile of metal, water leaked from a broken pipe making a river through the piles of debris. In the distance, he caught sight of a calico cat, sitting on a broken chair licking the mud from its coat He swallowed the lump in his throat and tried desperately to think rationally, but panic had him by the neck. *How the hell are we going to get out of here before we run out of food?*

"Are you okay, Branch?" Susie gave him a shake.

He patted her hand absently and dragged in a breath to steady his nerves. "Sure, I'm fine." Waving a hand toward the broken buildings, he winced. "I had no idea there was so much damage."

"What are we going to do?" Susie's voice trembled.

Branch started the engine. "We keep moving in the general direction of the Evacuation Center. I just hope the last bus made it in time."

"Then what?" She trembled against him. "We should try and get back before dark. I guess we'll need to find some dry stuff to light a fire?"

He needed to reassure her and shook his head. "I don't plan to stay away too long. I don't like leaving the old couple alone. As to a fire, I have a small gas cooker in the trunk of my car and everything we need for cooking. I even have a fishing rod. Unless we run out of water, we should be fine for a few days."

"Oh, look, that's not good." Susie pointed toward the west. "That's a mobile phone tower isn't it, or what's left of one. We'll have little chance of getting a signal now. I think we need a better plan than waiting for someone to come and help us."

Branch rubbed his chin. He'd wanted to give her hope, but she was an intelligent woman and could see the mess they were in. "We'll have to leave the Smithers behind, take some extra fuel and supplies, and try to find help, but it's too late to leave now. We'll head out first thing in the morning." He stared bleakly at the destruction. "The only good thing to come out of the hurricane is meeting you. I'm sure glad you're with me, darlin'." He squeezed her thigh. "Don't you worry I'll look after you."

"I *know* you will." Susie placed her trembling fingers over his hand. "I'm so glad I met you."

He desperately wanted to pull her into his arms kiss her and had done all day. Most of the women he knew would be hysterical by now. Susie, hell she was different, clumsy, sure but man, when push came to shove, she was right there beside him. Strange, he enjoyed being with her even in a disaster zone. That had to mean something. Yeah, Susie was one special lady, and one he could proudly take home to meet Grandma. Would Susie be interested in a relationship with him after surviving a hurricane or would she hightail it back to the UK? Then there was his career, the one he'd deliberately kept from her. Oh man, he was in deep shit. Reluctantly, he removed his hand and turned the motorcycle around. *I'll tell her once we are safe.* He cleared the strangling lump in his throat. "I'll check the immediate area to see if there are any survivors then we'll head back. It will be dark soon, and we'll need a safe, comfortable place to bed down tonight. We could sleep in the Mustang, but it will get very hot." He glanced over one shoulder but could not see her face. "The shower floor is the other option, as hard as hell but cooler."

"The shower floor, I think." Susie lifted her voice over the noise of the engine. "The toilet is close by, and we have our supplies. I think it will be okay once we sweep out the sand."

"Okay." He headed the Indian toward a pile of rubble in the distance and hoped like hell all the locals had taken shelter inland.

* * * *

After searching the debris for hours, Branch had given Susie a defeated shrug and turned the motorcycle toward the beach. The sun had dropped in the sky by the time Susie slipped off the seat. Muscles stiff, she staggered toward the amenities block.

"Did you find anything or anyone?" Mr. Smithers came out to greet them.

She leaned against the brick wall and shook her head. "Everything is gone it's the same as the beachfront for miles."

"We'll head out in the morning and see if we reach the evacuation center." Branch moved beside her. "We'll take supplies and keep on going until we find help, so don't worry if we don't return. The phone towers are down, so we have no chance of communicating, and I doubt we'll find a landline still working."

"Right you are." Mr. Smithers gave him a thin smile. "Best you make up a bed for the night. My wife has made a list of the supplies, so we'll divvy them up before you leave."

"I have a gas barbecue in the trunk of my car and everything we need so we can at least make a pot of coffee. There are heaps of cans of beans and the bread is still fresh." Branch smiled at him. "I'll find help, I promise."

"I'll get the things from the trunk and get the coffee started, if you give me the keys." Mr. Smithers nodded slowly. "You'll have work to do cleaning out the showers on your side."

"Okay." Branch handed him the keys. "You hang on to them, and use what you need."

Susie straightened. The idea of cleaning after an exhausting day was the last thing she needed. She headed for the women's side of the amenities block. "Let's get started."

Branch followed her inside and slid one muscular arm around her. He glanced around the room. "This place is in a mess, and I didn't think to put a broom or shovels in the trunk."

The tension seeped out of Susie at his touch, and she leaned into him sliding her thumb over his belt. "Do you have anything to open that cupboard?" She indicated toward the locked door. "I would imagine there are cleaning supplies in there we can use. There is one dry shower stall, and that's where I've stowed our bags."

"I have tools in the trunk of my car." He headed toward the entrance. "We might as well haul in the sleeping bags." Once outside, he led the way to the Mustang and turned to Mr. Smithers. "What's it like on your side of the building? We have a locked cupboard, and it might have a broom inside we can use."

"Our side is the same as yours I guess. Filled with garbage and sand." Mr. Smithers shrugged. "There is a similar cupboard in the men's showers. It would be easily opened with a claw hammer."

"I sure am happy I decided to fill my trunk with supplies. When I heard the hurricane warning, I recalled a story my grandpa told me. He did the same and saved our family from starvation after surviving a tornado." He chuckled. "But he didn't use a Mustang. He stored his supplies down an old well." He dug inside the trunk, pulled out rolled sleeping bags and handed them to her and Mr. Smithers. "Take these, I'll get the tools."

* * * *

Branch had both the storage doors open in minutes by using bolt cutters on the padlocks. Inside apart from cleaning utensils and containers of disinfectant, the shelves held toilet paper and liquid soap. A hose attached to a tap curled in one corner. He turned to Susie and shrugged. "I hope this isn't classed as looting."

"So do I." Susie snatched up a broom. "I guess if we offer to replace the stuff we use and replace the locks it will be okay." She pushed a pile of sand toward the entrance.

He picked up a broom and helped her. Half an hour later, hot, sweaty, and in desperate need of a shower, the area was finally clean. He stowed the broom and looked at Susie. Her flushed cheeks brought back a sweet reminder of their night of passion. His mouth watered at the memory of her skin sliding damp against his flesh. Her feminine fragrance had lodged a place in his mind, and her innocent need for him had curled around his heart. He wanted to run his hands over her silken skin and hear her moans of pleasure. Damn it, he needed someone like her in his life and his gut clenched at the idea of losing her. They needed a heart-to-heart before he fell so hard he doubted he would recover.

Clearing his throat, he strolled toward a shower stall. "I hope there's water. It will be cold, but I'd be happy just to wash off the grime." He turned on the faucet relieved when water burst from the pipes. The need to hold her again unleashed his tongue. "Coming? I'll keep you warm." *Oh, shit. Slow down, or she'll run for the hills.*

To his surprise, she met his gaze straight on with a hint of a challenge.

"We don't have any towels." Susie pushed a lock of dusty hair from her dirt-streaked face.

"Sure, we do." He indicated with his chin toward the two large bags he had rested on the sinks. "I have everything we need to keep us going for about a week, including a med kit."

"And a gun." She indicated toward his shoulder holster, and her mouth turned down in distaste. "Why do you carry a pistol?"

He shrugged. How could he explain? He had been born and raised on a farm in Texas. *Not* owning a firearm would be unusual. Remembering her upbringing, he softened his voice. "For safety. I'm guessing Mr. Smithers has one as well."

"We are the only people here." Susie shook her head dismay in her eyes. "I hate guns."

"I know you do, and I understand, but I've been around firearms all my life. Learning to shoot a rifle on a cattle ranch is a necessity." He slid one hand around her waist and pulled her close. "Darlin', we are alone now but what if a gang of thugs drop by to steal our supplies or worst try to rape you? In this type of situation, it can become a dog eat dog situation, and it's better to be safe." He brushed kisses over her cheek and inhaled her delicious scent. "Take a towel and the shampoo. The sooner we get clean, the faster we can eat." He pushed her gently toward the bags. "I need to make this place as safe as possible before we bed down for the night. I'll move the car close to the entrance then at least we'll have a warning. The alarm will go off if the car is rocked." He smiled. "I'll keep you safe. Now, how about those towels?"

"Okay." Susie unzipped the bag and peered inside then dragged out two towels. She tossed him the shampoo. "I'll shower dressed. I need to wash off some of this grime and hope my clothes will dry overnight. I only have one other pair of jeans and a couple of pairs of shorts in my backpack."

After placing the shampoo in the shower, he removed his shoulder holster then slipped the leather belt from his jeans. Grinning at her, he stepped under the water fully dressed. "Great idea to wash the outside first then the inside." He reached out and dragged her under the flow.

"You beast." She threw the towels on the bench giggling.

He washed his hair allowing the suds to flow down his clothes, and satisfied he had removed most of the dirt, stripped then noticed her watching him wide-eyed. *Oh, man, she is more innocent than I imagined.* He covered his groin with both hands and shrugged. "You're not embarrassed are you, darlin'? I believe you've already seen every inch of me."

"No not embarrassed" — she pulled her shirt over her head then unclipped her bra allowing her pale breasts to bounce free —

"impressed." She blushed to the roots of her hair. "You look even better in the daylight." She stepped under the flow and rinsed the soap from her hair.

He let out a long, relieved breath and waited for her to finish then turned off the shower. "Well, thank you, ma'am." He hooked his fingers into the waistband of her jeans and dragged her toward him. "You look mighty fine too."

CHAPTER SIX

All the problems of the day vanished the moment Susie looked into Branch's blue eyes. Pressed so intimately against his broad, muscular chest, nothing mattered but tasting his lips again. He moved his large warm hands up her back but made no move to kiss her as if he wanted her to make the first move. She wet her lips, and his attention moved to her mouth then flicked back to her, and his pupils dilated with passion. She remembered his creed about not going where he wasn't welcome and lifted up on her toes to lick a path across his lips.

"Oh, darlin'." Branch bent his head to claim her mouth in a long, passionate kiss.

She sighed against his mouth and melted into him kissing him back with passion. He used his tongue to explore her mouth leaving her knees weak. She clung to his neck wanting him deep inside her, and when he pulled back, she dragged him down and nibbled the corners of his smile. "I want you." The words spilled out before she could stop them. What would he think of her now? Not wanting to die a virgin, she had practically begged him to make love to her during the storm. Their long night of passion had unleashed a restlessness in her only he could cure. Drawing in a steadying breath, she tried to step away from him, but he held her close. "I'm sorry. You must think I'm forward coming on to you like a wanton hussy especially after what we've been through. I don't know what's got into me."

He chuckled low and sexy, and the sound made her insides turn to mush.

"You sure don't act sleazy, so wanton hussy is way off the mark, darlin', and the urges you feel are normal." He stared into her eyes for a long moment and sighed. "I want you too but not in here. It's no place to make love to a lady." He moved his hands to the button on her jeans then slid down the zipper. "First, let me help you out of your wet clothes and then we'll do this right." He pushed jeans and panties down to her knees then met her gaze again. "I was your first lover, wasn't I?"

Her cheeks burned with embarrassment, and she avoided his stare. "I'm sorry. I should have told you."

When he cupped her chin in his large hand and brushed a kiss over her lips, she looked at him with every nerve ending burning with desire. His lips curled into a cute smile, but his eyes held a tenderness.

"You gave me a special gift." He rubbed the pad of his thumb over her cheek. "I am humbled you chose me. I've grown attached to you in a short time, Susie, and I'm not just talking the talk to get into your pants." He sighed and slipped his arms around her waist. "I want to forget the chaos outside and make love to you all night again. You make me insatiable, and I can't wait to taste you again."

A shiver of awareness curled around her damp folds, and she stepped out of the jeans leaning on him for support. The next second, he swept her into his muscular arms and carried her outside the cubicle and down to the place he had made cozy for the night. He lowered her to her feet, and her heart pounded in anticipation.

He turned away to collect the towels then gave her a slow sexy smile "You are so darn pretty." He laid the towels over the sleeping bags then reached into his bag and pulled out a strip of condoms. He cupped her chin and brushed a tender kiss across her lips. "Come here." He pulled her close and took her mouth in a possessive claiming.

Disorientated by the waves of passion igniting every nerve ending, she slid her hands into his damp hair and pressed against him. Her hard nipples grazed against his hot flesh in tingles of desire. She moaned at the delicious taste of him flowing over her taste buds and hungrily drank in his flavor. When he walked her backward, and she heard the click of the door locking, she broke the kiss. "Oh, gosh I hope nobody walks in on us."

"They won't." Branch lifted her, and her back hit the soft towels. "But they'll hear us. Sound travels in these open areas but don't worry by the aroma of fresh coffee the Smithers are cooking some ways away." He lowered to her side then ran the tips of his rough fingers down her chest then circled one straining nipple. "Dear Lord, you are beautiful. I love your nipples, like cherries on ice cream and your skin, so soft. The dimples in your cheeks match the ones on your bottom, and I want to kiss them all over and over again."

With his gaze fixed on her, he trailed his warm fingers over her flesh to cup one breast. She arched and a smile curved his full mouth. He lowered his head and circled her erect tip with his hot, wet tongue. She gasped rolling in the divine sensations, and when he suckled, she cupped the back of his neck wanting the feeling to go on forever. When he moved to the other breast, she tossed her head. "I can't stand this much pleasure, Branch."

"Do you want me to stop?" He lifted his head and licked his wet lips. "Or do you want me to taste more of you." He slid one hand down to her folds, and one finger dipped inside. "Mmm, you are so wet, and your hard nub needs my undivided attention." He swirled his finger, and her hips rose to meet his caress as if they had a mind of their own.

Trying to break out of the sexual spell he weaved over her, she pushed words out of her mouth. "I don't want you to stop, but you make me feel like I'm going to burst."

He chuckled low and sexy. "That's the plan, darlin'." He kissed a wet path down her stomach, then buried his face between her thighs and parted her folds.

Biting back a scream of delight, she dug her fingers into his shoulders and rolled her hips with each swirl of his tongue. Tension balled, and she craved release, but before she fell over the edge, he lifted his head. She heard the tear of paper, and she closed her eyes to give him privacy to suit up. The next moment his mouth came down on her lips, sliding over her demanding a response. She opened her thighs, and he slid over her not breaking the kiss. When he entered her, hard and so darn hot, she moaned her approval and lifted her knees to lock her ankles around his waist. He pushed up and stared down at her then rolled his hips.

"So tight, you are milking me, honey." He bent to press kisses up her neck.

She swallowed hard, not sure if he was complaining. "I'm sorry."

He stopped moving and stared down at her with a perplexed expression.

"*Sorry?* Don't be sorry, you are a perfect fit for me in every way." He bent to press kisses to her breasts. "Mmm, you taste like peaches." He pushed in so deep she moaned her appreciation. "You like that, huh?"

Unable to speak, she clung to him on a ride into paradise. His warm breath brushed her cheek, and with each stroke, the passion mounted, climbing, climbing, into a spiral of ultimate joy. She shattered trembling, her climax extended by his deep thrusts until he let out a long moan and rolled to one side drawing her with him. She gazed at his handsome face, cheeks flushed from exhaustion. His long sinful lashes brushed his cheeks, and his breath came in long gasps. When he opened his eyes, the look he gave her melted her heart.

"Oh, baby, you'll be the death of me. I want you again already. I can't get enough, but from the way your stomach is growling I have been very negligent at caring for my woman." He slipped one hand around her waist and nuzzled her neck. "Give me a few minutes to catch my breath, and we'll go and see what the Smithers have found to eat."

"Okay." She snuggled against him. The thought of food the last thing on her mind.

Their time together had been amazing but what would happen after they left Florida and what would she do now she had nowhere to live? The idea of not seeing him again tugged at her heart. In a short time, she had developed a huge crush on him and become almost dependent. The idea of losing his friendship worried her, and she let out a long sigh. He opened one blue eye and smiled at her.

"Bored with me already?" He touched her cheek.

Her face grew hot, and she swallowed hard. "No, of course not. I was wondering what happens next. I mean, as soon as we leave here and go our separate ways, I guess I won't see you again."

I don't want to lie to her, but I have no choice. Branch drew a deep breath and commended his soul to God. "I don't want to lose contact with you. In fact, I'd love to continue getting to know you, but my life is complicated."

"What do you mean?" Susie frowned and examined him closely. "Are you in trouble with the law?"

He laughed. "Hell no." He smoothed a lock of her blonde hair behind one ear. "Now my vacation is over I'll be working away from home a lot. Trying to establish any kind of a relationship with you will be difficult."

She raised up on one elbow and eyed him critically. "I do understand, but these days with the internet, people can keep in touch. What is it you do for a living? You haven't mentioned anything other than the ranch."

He cleared his throat searching his brain for an excuse. "I er . . . we've been kind of busy with the hurricane and all." He ran the pad of his thumb over her bottom lip. "Does my working away from home make that much of a difference to you, Susie?"

"No. Long-distance relationships do work sometimes." She sighed again and glanced up at the ceiling. "How will you find me after we leave this place? I don't even have a phone number to give you let alone an address."

His heart ached to see the uncertainty in her beautiful eyes. "I'm not planning on leaving your side for a while." He waited for her to look at him. "And I'll make sure you have my number and address just in case we're separated. Okay?"

"Okay."

He held her close for a few minutes longer then coaxed her to get dressed. "It will be dark soon, and we need to eat. I'll pack enough to keep us going on our trip, but I have limited space on the motorcycle." He smiled at her. "Put as many supplies as you can in your backpack, especially water."

"I guess we'll be leaving at first light, well, as soon as we've eaten breakfast?" Susie moved supplies from their survival packs into her backpack. She turned and smiled at him but worry clouded her expression. "I noticed Mrs. Smithers has rigged up a washing line. I'll take our things outside and hang them up. In this heat, they should be dry by the morning." She turned to collect the wet washing, and he caught her around the waist.

"I'm *not* leaving you alone." He turned her to face him. "You have my word. I like you, darlin', and I want to see where this crazy relationship takes us. I've not met a woman quite like you before, and if necessary, I'll put work on the backburner for a while. Will that be okay?"

"Yes, of course. I get it, really I do." Susie's mouth quivered and curled up at the edges. "It doesn't make any difference to me, what you do. I liked you as a beach bum and being a cattle rancher or whatever is fine. Not that I especially like cows — but for you, I'll give it a try." She snorted with laughter.

He let her go then turned to collect his backpack. When she returned, he slid one arm around her waist and drew her close." I know you're worried, but if you can't contact your father, you're coming home with me — okay?"

"Thanks." Susie beamed at him. "I would love to see your ranch."

"Well, before you head off to the hills, you'd better eat." Mrs. Smithers waddled toward them carrying two plates. "There's plenty of food, so eat up before it spoils."

"It looks wonderful." Branch grinned at her. "Nothing better than a pile of beans."

* * * *

The following morning, Susie stretched in an effort to relieve the pain in her back from sleeping on a very hard floor. She'd woken half sprawled across Branch's chest, her tee shirt hiked up, and his hand cupping one breast as if claiming her. Glancing up she stared straight into his amused blue gaze, and her cheeks grew hot.

"I could get used to waking up with you in my arms, darlin'." Branch teased her nipple between finger and thumb. "Mmm, you are so receptive to my touch, but loving will have to wait. We need to be on our way." He slowly untangled his long body and rolled onto his knees. "You get dressed, and I'll put on a pot of coffee. The bags are all packed, and as soon as we've eaten, we can be on our way."

She pulled down her shirt and tried to ignore the throbbing ache between her thighs. He had become an addiction and one she did not intend to give up. Looking up at his impressive frame, she smiled. "I'll be five minutes. Do you know where the evacuation center is located?"

"I know the general direction. The bus that picked up the people from my building was heading for the Deltona High School." Branch offered his hand and effortlessly pulled her to her feet. "With the landmarks missing, we'll keep moving in that direction and hope the building is still standing." He sat on the bench and pulled on socks and boots. "I'll leave you to get dressed." His hot gaze drifted over her bare legs and his full mouth curved into a sexy grin. "I can't believe we've been through a hurricane, lost everything and yet my mind is filled with you. It's as if nothing else matters." He bent to brush a chaste kiss across her lips and let out a long sigh. "You are bewitching me, Susie Blake."

She gaped after him, taking in the width of broad shoulders and noticing a small scar over one hip, a white line marring the perfect tan. Shaking her head, she forced her mind to concentrate on the job at hand and gathered up the sleeping bags before taking a quick wash and dressing. She hurried outside, dragging a hairbrush through the tangles in her hair to find Branch and Mr. and Mrs. Smithers chatting around the barbecue. The smell of coffee greeted her, and she took the cup Mrs. Smithers offered her. "Thank you. I'm going to miss drinking coffee on our journey."

"Well, then it's lucky I have a thermos you can take with you. At least you'll have something to drink at lunchtime. Branch said he would keep going until he found help, so I don't expect you back here again." Mrs. Smithers moved closer to her husband. "I hope you find someone soon. I'm not sure how many nights I can sleep on the cold floor."

Susie patted her arm. "No, it is not very comfortable, but I guess it's better than sleeping in the open."

"It's cold beans for breakfast, I'm afraid." Branch handed her a small can of baked beans and a fork. "I've eaten my share, so I'll go and get ready then collect our bags." He strolled toward the amenities block.

Susie sat on the ground to eat her breakfast, and Mrs. Smithers sat beside her in a companionable way. She glanced at the old woman. "I gather this hurricane is a lot worse than the others that have been through this area recently. How long did it take help to arrive the last time this happened?"

"Not long at all but the damage wasn't as widespread." Mrs. Smithers waved a hand toward the demolished buildings. "I expect we'll see helicopters doing a search of the area within the next few hours. My husband and I went down to the beach at daybreak and scratched 'help' in the sand. If they come this way they'll see it for sure."

"What a good idea. You should have woken us to help you." Susie ate the last mouthful of beans and washed it down with coffee before getting to her feet. "I'd better go and help Branch. He said we needed to be away from here as soon as possible to preserve daylight."

"No need." Mr. Smithers indicated behind her with his chin. "There he is now."

Minutes later, she sat astride the motorcycle with bags bulging with supplies and waved goodbye to the old couple. The idea of leaving them alone worried her, but they had no choice. As the motorcycle roared into life, she clung to Branch's waist and rested her cheek against his broad back. As Branch moved the Indian through the piles of debris with skill, she kept her gaze fixed on Mr. and Mrs. Smithers. The old couple stood and waved until they disappeared from sight. A knot of worry curled in her gut. *I hope we find help soon.*

Utter desolation met them at every turn, and the further Branch drove the more confused he became. After an hour, he glanced down at the fuel gauge and grimaced. Driving so slow used more gas, and by his estimation, they would not make it back to the beach if anything went wrong. Ahead, he recognized the outside of the local library standing untouched amidst the chaos. He wanted to punch the air with joy. Now he had his bearings, he headed toward the building and discovered the adjoining street virtually untouched by the storm. Relief flooded over him, and he increased his speed easily avoiding the rubbish littering the road. The evacuation center was less than ten miles away, and in the distance, he spotted a group of people strolling along the sidewalk. At last, an emergency response team had arrived. He slowed the motorcycle to greet them, but the next moment one of the men hurled a brick through a plate glass shop front window. A group of looters ran inside, and the rest of the young men spread out across the road waiting for them. He caught a flash of metal as one of the gang pulled a knife. Anger gripped him, quickly followed by panic for Susie's safety. The youths would have weapons, and he sure did not intend to hang around to chat. He turned his head and raised his voice over the motorcycle's engine. "Hang on tight. We need to get out of here fast."

He revved the engine and let out the clutch, but the vintage Indian spluttered and died. Branch glanced over his shoulder and froze in horror. Not one hundred yards away, the gang members had broken into a run pounding down the center of the road toward them.

CHAPTER SEVEN

B ranch had rebuilt this vehicle from the frame up and understood every one of its eccentricities. He cursed under his breath and tried to keep his head into the now. He opened the throttle and gave the engine a few cranks to clear the fuel line. The gang bore down on them with speed and had covered fifty yards in seemingly Olympic record time. Saying a prayer, he closed the throttle, and to his relief, the motor kicked into life. "Hang on like a leach and keep your head down. Look over my shoulder so you can gauge which way I'm turning. You'll need to move with me."

"Okay." Susie closed her arms around him and gripped his belt. "Go!"

He took off at speed, dodging fallen trees and piles of wet garbage. A shot rang out, and he ducked over the handlebars, taking Susie with him. She clung to him trembling and squeezed him so tight, he could hardly breathe. Getting out of the line of fire was a priority, and if they could make it to the next block before the gang rounded the corner, they might lose them in the maze of back streets and buildings in the area. He tore down the street heading toward the crossroads at breakneck speed. They rounded the corner fast and with a screech of metal, the motorcycle's pedals hit the blacktop sending a spray of blue sparks into the air. Engine revving, he barely righted the powerful machine before skidding past the broken facade of a building strewn across the road and flying down a back alley before emerging onto another street. He slid the powerful machine through a patch of mud barely missing an abandoned car. Susie's scream of fear broke through the noise, and he slowed to glance over one shoulder. No one followed, but the gang would be able to hear them. He kept the revs of the engine to a minimum and peered through the wrecked buildings. If the Indian run out of fuel, they would be toast, but he had managed to get a fair distance between them and the looters. If they kept going, the gang had no hope of catching them but to do that, he would need to find a supply of gas. Finding a safe place to hide with available fuel would be a problem. If they lucked out, they had maybe ten to twenty minutes before the gang caught up with them.

"Why are those men shooting at us?" Susie's voice came out in a high-pitched squeal.

Branch squeezed her hand in an effort to calm her. Hysterical and screaming, she would be a problem. "They are looting the area and probably want the Indian." He forced his voice to come out calm and soothing. "We need to be as quiet as possible. Sound travels in empty streets. Right now, we are safe, okay?"

"What are we going to do now?" Susie brushed at her tear-streaked cheeks.

"Right now, I'm not sure." He shrugged trying to appear nonchalant as if gangs armed with weapons chased him on a daily basis. "I'll think of something. Don't worry, darlin'. I won't let anything happen to you."

Branch glanced around to get his bearings and searched the buildings for a place to hide. The library had an underground parking lot, and people may have left their cars behind. He headed back toward the building and aimed the motorcycle down the ramp and into the dark interior. Using his headlamp, he surveyed a few cars covered with dust and wondered if anyone had remained in the building. He noticed an old Ford parked in one corner and turned off the motorcycle's engine. The notion of damaging someone's car flashed through his mind. *Desperate times call for desperate measures.* Once people had returned, he would come back, find the owner, and buy him a new car. "I have a pint bottle of gas in the saddlebags, but we'll need more. I'll have to steal some from that old car. Jump off. I have a hose and pump in the saddlebag."

Susie slid off the seat and glanced nervously at the entrance. She turned to him, her face sheet-white and offered him a tentative smile that came over more as a grimace. "I'm scared."

He pulled her into his arms. "You are the bravest woman I know."

"I'm trying."

He found her mouth and used his tongue to open her lips. When she sighed into his mouth, he devoured her, tasting and exploring. When she melted against him pressing her hard nipples into his chest, he deepened the kiss and squeezed her ass. He needed more time alone with her to show her his true self. Once she discovered his fame, everything would change. He wanted her, and it had been a long time since he'd had a woman interested in him for being plain old Branch and not the singer with a multimillion-dollar empire behind him. Soon they would be out of this hell, and he would have to explain about his career. Dear God, even with a gang close by he wanted this moment to go on forever, confessing he was famous would break the erotic spell woven between them. He cared for her, and by the way she was kissing him back and making that delicious little moaning sound, she liked him fine too. Raising his head, he stared into her eyes and sighed. "You do things to me, darlin', and I don't want you to stop." He nibbled her bottom lip. "This is not just sex between us. I'm falling for you big time, and it scares the hell outta me."

Her face went a beautiful shade of pink, but she didn't look away.

"I think you're pretty special too but don't be scared. I don't bite . . . unless you want me to." She brushed a kiss over his lips. "As much as I'd like to crawl into the back seat of a car with you right now and test your theory, I guess you should try and find some gas before the gang discovers our hiding place."

Reluctantly he stepped away and smiled. "I prefer the first option."

"Me too." Susie giggled and touched her lips. "I'll go and keep watch."

He touched her arm and offered her a reassuring squeeze. "I doubt they'll find us down here but just in case stay out of sight. Don't remove your helmet. If they start shooting again, it might save your life." He pulled out his cell phone. "Take this and check for a signal."

"Okay." She turned hesitantly away then moved slowly along the wall and made her way up the exit ramp.

Legs trembling with lust more than fear, Susie edged her way up the ramp and keeping her back to the wall did a turkey peek out the entrance. The road was empty. She glanced back at Branch. He was bending over an old car with a screwdriver in one hand prying open the gas tank. Her mouth watered at the sight of him. He was so damn sexy, and his jeans had hidden nothing of his arousal for her. The attraction between them was real, he had admitted as much and getting a man to declare he liked her this early in a relationship had to mean something. The idea of making love again made her pussy tingle. She pushed away the thought and tried to concentrate on getting to safety. "All clear. Any luck finding some gas?"

"Yeah, and we don't need much to fill the tank." Branch's voice echoed in the empty lot. "We'll be out of here in five." He slid one end of the hose inside the tank. "I'm sure glad I had this pump inside my survival kit, it sure beats sucking the gas through a tube."

The smell of petroleum wafted toward her. She turned her attention back to the street flicking her gaze from one corner to the other, looking for any sign of movement. An eerie quiet surrounded the deserted buildings. A line of four apartment complexes torn apart by the storm with gaping maws and broken windows like empty eye sockets stood beside others untouched as if the hurricane had selected which ones to destroy. Between the twisted metal, bricks and mortar, the blacktop glistened with broken glass as if the sky had rained diamonds. The only noise came from the wind rustling through the debris and rolling balls of paper around like tumbleweeds, no birdsong, nothing. It was as if Branch and her, had been the only people, apart from the gang terrorizing them, to survive Armageddon. Her skin pebbled in fear. What if the looters headed along the beachfront and found the Smithers? She slid Branch's cell phone from her pocket and checked the signal again. "There's still no signal, how many towers do you think were destroyed in the storm?"

"I have no idea, but as we haven't seen any choppers or any kind of assistance yet, I gather the damage is widespread. I hope the emergency shelter is still standing. If it's not, we'll have to keep going until we find help." Branch pushed the Indian toward her. "Take a drink and if you need to pee, duck behind the car because once I fire up the beast, I'm not stopping until we reach safety. I need to get help to the Smithers before that gang discovers their location."

Susie handed him the cell phone then rubbed her arms. "I was thinking the same thing" She took the bottle of water he offered, took a few sips then handed it back. "I'm good, let's go."

"Okay." Branch swung onto the motorcycle then kicked it into life. "Jump on, hold on to me and don't let go. The road ahead looks pretty bad, so I'll be swerving a lot." He tightened the strap on his helmet and smiled. "Not long now, sweetheart."

The rumble of the motorcycle's engine bounced off the buildings, booming with each gear change. Susie clung to Branch. Under her palms, his heart pounded and his muscles tensed. Her confidence in his skill at riding the vintage Indian had risen by the second. The way he maneuvered through the piles of destruction amazed her. She learned very quickly to hold her body against him and move as one through the curves. As they reached the main highway, the hurricane damage decreased. Instead of bricks, leaves and shredded palm trees covered the road. When Branch pushed the motorcycle to top speed, the wind cut through her clothes and whipped her hair out of the helmet and across her face. Miles flashed by, and in no time they coasted into the parking lot of the shelter. Outside the building, people milled about, faces drawn with anxiety, some with phones pressed to their ears. At last, they would be able to get help.

Without saying a word to her, Branch parked the motorcycle, dragged off his helmet then pulled out his phone. She listened in amazement as he barked orders to someone he called, Kade.

"I want our choppers in the air, like yesterday. Find out where you can land, there must be somewhere near here, I can hear others close by." Branch rubbed his chin. "Call me when you're five minutes away. I have to report the damage along the beach to whoever is in charge, and I'll need immediate assistance for an elderly couple with a looting gang in the area. I'll give you the coordinates when you get here. No, better still, I'll show you, or you will have difficulty finding them, the hurricane destroyed all the local landmarks. See you soon." He disconnected and turned to her. "Help is on the way."

Susie slid off the seat and rubbed her backside. "Thank goodness." She removed her helmet and handed it to him. "Do you know someone with a helicopter?"

"Yeah, we have them on the ranch. I was speaking to my brother, Kade." Branch collected their belongings from the saddlebags.

"Thanks." Susie slung her backpack over one shoulder and indicated with her chin toward a few familiar faces. "I can see some of the people from my building. It looks like everyone got here okay."

"That's great." Branch looked into the distance as if deciding to confide in her. His Adam's apple moved up and down, and he drew a deep breath then let it out slowly. "Wait before you rush off, we need to talk. I should have been honest with you before, Susie, I—"

Her heart sunk to her boots. "You're married, aren't you?" She held up both hands like a cop stopping traffic. "It's okay. I *understand*. We both thought it was the end of the world. I won't tell anyone I even know you, I promise." *I have to get away from him.* She looked frantically for the entrance to the shelter and turned to go.

"I'm *not* married, and I'm not the type of man who cheats on his wife." Branch clutched her arm and turned her to face him. "Oh, darlin', I've haven't met anyone like you before, and I was too darn chicken to tell you the truth about me. I didn't want to spoil what I had with you. It was so good to be normal for a few days, but now we're here, people will recognize me, and you'll probably kick me to the curb for being dishonest." He dashed a hand through his thick unruly hair and stared at her with such a forlorn expression her heart twisted.

Unsure, she took a small step backward. "Are you a serial killer or something?"

His laughter made people turn and gape at them. Susie blinked. "Well?"

"I have been in a few brawls, but I haven't killed anyone yet." Branch's grin slashed brilliant white across his tanned face. "I'm a Country and Western singer."

Stymied, she lifted her chin. "What has that to do with anything? Oh, my God. It's because I hate country music, isn't it? Is that a deal breaker for a relationship?" Her mind reeled at the implications. "I guess, I could get to like it, I haven't heard the latest tunes. I think Jim Reeves has a nice voice. My neighbor used to play all his songs really loud."

"Jim Reeves, huh? You haven't heard *my* songs, and most people seem to like them fine." He pulled her into his arms, and his warm breath brushed her neck. "I sing about love and breaking hearts, but that's not the problem. I can't go anywhere in public without being recognized, and that means little or no privacy. I love my fans, but I know many relationships rarely survive fame." He pushed his long fingers through her hair. "That's why I hid in my dad's apartment. I needed a break, and I could sneak around unnoticed. Meeting you as a normal person meant what we had together was real and not influenced by who I am." He waved a hand toward the crowd gathering out front of the building. "That is going to change in the next few minutes. Will you be able to cope and does this make a difference to us?"

"No, to me, you are Branch, the cowboy I met on the beach. All this crazy fame stuff is a different world and one I don't give a damn about, and it doesn't change my perception of you." She touched his face then looped her arms around his neck. "I've nearly drowned, been through a hurricane, and escaped a gang of thugs. I'm sure surviving the wrath of your fans will be a piece of cake."

"Okay, darlin'." Branch kissed the tip of her nose, stepped back and offered his hand. "Hold on tight because the next few hours is going to be crazy."

* * * *

He was not joking. The moment they approached the front door of the shelter a crowd of people surrounded them, and even secure under Branch's strong arm, the push and pull of a mass of people yelling questions terrified Susie. She took a firm hold of his belt and kept her head down. To her surprise, he took his time and answered their questions all the time insisting he needed to make a report to the man in charge. Eventually, he eased her through an office door, and a kindly yet rather frazzled looking man by the name of Gary Harvard smiled at her then waved her into a seat.

Sandwiches and coffee seemed to arrive instantly, and as Branch explained the situation, she ate slowly. The cold meat sandwiches tasted like nectar, and the instant coffee smelled like the finest roast. "This is wonderful. I hadn't realized I was so hungry."

"My pleasure." Gary Harvard turned back to Branch. "I'll keep Miss Blake in my office when you leave, or she'll be harassed by your fans."

"Thanks, I think the fans were a bit of a shock to her, but she is the strongest woman I know. Once I've left, they'll calm down. Having someone like me around only causes a nuisance in this kind of situation. I'm sure you agree?" Branch flicked her a gaze. "My main concern is getting the Smithers out of danger. I'll have another of my choppers on the way to lend assistance." Branch sipped his coffee and grimaced. "It comes with two pilots so will be available for transporting around the clock."

When Branch's phone blasted out a saucy ringtone, she turned to look at him, but he'd jumped to his feet. He squeezed her shoulder. "That's my ride. I have to go."

She swallowed a mouthful of food. "What? We've just arrived."

"Our choppers have landed. I'm going out with Kade to find the old couple." Branch squeezed her shoulder. "You'll be safe here. Try to get in touch with your father. I'm guessing he'll be worried about you. Tell him, my people will make sure you get safely to Hawaii." He gave her a crooked grin and handed her the keys to the Indian. "Take care of my motorcycle. Gary will find a nice safe place to store it until I can arrange for a pickup."

"Okay." A wave of panic hit her making her lip quiver. "Stay safe."

"Darlin', 'safe' is my middle name." He strode out of the office and disappeared into the crowd of people.

"Well, we'll give the folks a few minutes to settle down then you can show me where Mr. Durham parked his motorcycle." Gary folded his hands on the desk. "I have a garage out back, it will be safe enough there."

Susie forced her lips into a smile. "Maybe while we're waiting you can tell me all about Branch Durham, and by the way that's not *just* a motorcycle, it's a 1934 Indian, and his most prized possession."

"I gather you are not aware of Branch's notoriety? He is a favorite of the ladies." Gary raised both brows. "His latest album is sitting number one on the charts as we speak."

"I had no idea he was famous or a singer. I'm new to the USA. We met just before the storm hit and I guess he didn't have time to mention his career. He was too busy trying to save everyone."

"Well then, I better get you another cup of coffee." Gary pushed to his feet and waved to a woman in the foyer. He turned back to Susie. "Let me see, how I can explain where Branch Durham fits into the music world. Have you heard of Elvis?"

CHAPTER EIGHT

With the hum of an old air conditioner rattling in the corner, Susie listened to the story of Branch's successful life with amazement. With twenty platinum albums, the singer-songwriter was, according to Gary, a chart-topper worldwide. No wonder people mobbed him the moment they arrived. The way Branch handled the crowd as if he had all the time in the world, made her appreciate his professionalism. In fact, he'd acted with confidence the entire time she'd known him, and she thought it was his unique natural charm, not one acquired from years of practice. Why the Smithers had neglected to mention anything about his fame astounded her, but if they had been his father's friends, they would have known Branch for some time. Astonished, she leaned forward in her chair digesting every detail of his remarkable life. She had to agree Branch had sex appeal in spades. No wonder she had fallen for his charismatic allure. In fact, fame aside he must have been born to make women swoon with his good looks and his voice. "I honestly have not heard of him, but Country and Western music isn't my thing. He saved me from drowning then the storm hit, and we were too busy trying to survive to discuss his life. He did mention something about living on a ranch in Texas and a bit about his family. Branch is a very nice man, and he took care of me. I hope being alone with him won't upset anyone. He said he isn't married, is that true?"

"From what I've read in the media, I don't think Branch hangs around women long enough to form a relationship. I hope you didn't get bewitched by the Durham charm. He is well known to be a player with the ladies." Gary gave her a pitying smile. "I don't think he's the marrying kind."

No wonder he conveniently forgot to give me his phone number. She stared at the steaming mug in her hands allowing Branch's last words to percolate in her mind. He had told her to call her father, and *his people* would arrange the trip to Hawaii. In fact, he had not mentioned he would be returning to collect her. Although, he had made sure his precious Indian motorcycle was safe and secure. She squeezed the cup until her knuckles went white. *He's not coming back.*

"Are you okay?" Gary cleared his throat.

"I'm fine." She lifted her gaze to him.

"Do you want me to call your father now? I'll need a contact number for your next of kin and some details for our records."

A tight band squeezed her chest at the thought of losing Branch. "Yes, please call him. I have his number."

She pulled the small purse containing her passport, credit cards, and address book out of her pocket. After giving him her details and her father's cell phone number, she buried her nose in the coffee cup in an attempt to appear nonchalant. Her face grew hot with embarrassment. Likely, Gary had read the situation between her and Branch. Her knight in shining armor had extricated himself out of her life in one very smooth and no doubt, well-practiced move. She snorted in disgust at her stupidity. As if a famous singer would be interested in a relationship with a fat clumsy idiot, plus the fact Branch would believe she had the morals of an alley cat. She had begged him to make love to her and being family orientated, he would not risk introducing someone with a potentially undesirable background to his grandma.

"Susie?" Gary held out the phone.

She took the phone. "Hi, Dad. Yes, I'm fine. The hurricane destroyed the condominium. I've lost everything and need a place to stay."

"Don't come here, it's not necessary. Daphne, that's your stepmother if you recall, owns a nice apartment in Dallas. We had planned to put it on the market, but it will suit you just fine until we rebuild the condominium."

"That will take at least a year. I don't have enough money to support myself in the meantime. I was relying on the wages from my job as your manager. I'll need to look for something straight away, and I doubt anyone will hire me without credentials and wearing the clothes I have right now. I'll have to replace my references, and that will take weeks." Susie swallowed hard, her savings would not last long after replacing her wardrobe, and she would need a car.

"Not to worry. The insurance will cover most of what you have lost, and replace my car. I have your bank account details, and I'll pay you what we agreed until you find a job. Daphne's car is in the garage. We'll have the title signed over to you. It's the least we can do after what you've been through."

Susie sighed with relief. "Thank you. Give me the address. I want to leave here as soon as possible. Can you contact the building supervisor and get me a key?"

"Everything will be organized by the time you arrive. The building supervisor is a woman by the name of Amelia Banks. I'm sure I can persuade her to pick you up at the airport. If not, I'll call you back with the address. There are seven flights a day out of Tampa. Give me a call and the time you expect to arrive at the airport and I'll arrange the flight. It will take you a couple of hours to fly from Tampa to Dallas."

"Okay. Thanks, Dad, I'll call you back in a little while." She handed Gary the phone. "I need to get to Tampa Airport. My father has a place in Dallas, and I can stay there."

"That's good." Gary smiled. "We have a bus heading that way in about an hour. You will have time to shower and change. Do you have a set of clothes in your backpack?"

Susie nodded, but the idea of setting off alone again made her stomach ache. "Is there anyone heading to Dallas do you know? I would appreciate the company."

"There are four couples heading back to Texas, so they'll help you find your way around."

She stared at him uncomprehending. "Texas? I'm heading for Dallas."

"Dallas is in Texas." Gary frowned. "I know Branch lives there. Is that going to be a problem?"

Only if Branch thinks I'm stalking him. She pushed the idea from her mind. The chances of bumping into him in the street were less than zero. He had been a nice diversion and a lover she would not forget, but he could not be anything more than a pleasant memory. No matter how many times his sweet words replayed in her mind, she had to forget him and move on with her life. She cleared her throat. "No, of course not. May I use your phone again? My father has offered to book me a flight."

* * * *

Branch turned his Stetson around in one hand and picked off the dead leaves before pushing it back on his head. He had rescued his hat from the front seat of his Mustang. In the rush to leave earlier, he left the window open, and now the car interior needed a good clean. As the chopper moved over the altered landscape, he glanced at the widespread devastation and wondered if he would ever manage to get the vehicle home. The Smithers had been in good spirits when he arrived and after a stopover to arrange for relatives to collect them, they had dropped them on top of a hotel in Tampa. The moment they had become airborne the radio had lit up with requests for assistance.

After six hours of transporting injured people to hospitals, exhausted, Branch sighed and leaned back in the seat of the chopper. He needed a good meal, and a long sleep — his preference after a long sexy shower with his girl. His mind went to Susie, and he hoped she had contacted her father, although from what she had told him, he was little more than a stranger to her.

The idea of leaving her with her father worried him but pushing her into a relationship with him after knowing her for a few days would be foolish. At first, he had made grand plans to take her home with him and introduce her to Grandma as his girl, but Susie was so darn innocent. Worse still, he had acted like a teenager by giving into his lust when deep down, he should have known better. Susie was a special lady and not a one-night-stand. Now he had the added problem of his career and all that entailed. The lack of privacy alone could ruin their fledgling relationship. If she decided not to go to her father, he would find her a place to stay and do the right thing by asking her out on dates. He would take it slowly and not push her if she needed time to adjust to the idea of being with him. Leaving her for six hours or so would have given her time to think, and if she wanted to go to her father, he would take her personally.

He smiled remembering their crazy time together. Their frantic lovemaking had been spectacular. She would be worth waiting for, and he had confidence he could win her affection. After all, the press insisted he had expertise in pleasing women. He could not remember being so happy as if he'd found his soulmate at last. Now all he had to do was convince her to overlook the fame and see him as plain old Branch. After all, he was the same person she had begged to make love to her. He could not blame his reputation for influencing her decision. Perhaps when she knew him better, she would look past the image, and see the cowboy she first met on the beach.

"I'll need to rest before we take off again." Kade's voice came through his headphones. "Then we'll have to head home. Your manager has been raising hell all week. He has some crazy idea you've forgotten you leave on tour on Tuesday."

Bemused, Branch rubbed his chin. "Well, I've had a few things on my mind, and somehow the tour was way down on my survival list."

"Call him before he has a coronary." Kade snorted in obvious glee. "He'll want to know you haven't damaged that pretty face of yours."

"Dirk is the last person on my 'need to call' list." He sighed with relief as the shelter came into view. "Grandma will want to hear from me first."

"I told her you were fine." Kade dropped the chopper into a football field set aside for emergency vehicles and dragged off his headphones. "We'll check-in and pick up your lady friend then I'm heading for the closest hotel with a helipad."

Branch chuckled and got ready to leave. "And the biggest steak on the menu — maybe two."

After dragging his weary bones back through the milling crowds of people hanging around the shelter, he reached Gary's office with Kade following close behind. The smell of sweat inside the room seemed to permeate every breath of humid air. He glanced around and not seeing Susie smiled at Gary. "I've come to pick up my girl."

"I put her in the storage locker out back." Gary pushed to his feet and picked up a bunch of keys from the desk. "I thought it would be some time before you could make arrangements to collect her." He moved around the desk. "It's just outside the back door, no need to go back through the hall."

Branch pushed back his hat and scratched his sweat-laden head in disbelief then glared at the tired man. "Why would you put Susie in a storage locker?"

"Susie? Good Lord, no. I thought you meant your motorcycle." Gary chuckled then his kindly face creased into a frown. "I'm afraid Susie isn't here. She took the bus to Tampa Airport some hours ago. She called her father, and he arranged a flight for her."

Desolation hit Branch in a rush. Unable to grasp the situation he gaped at him. "She left? Holy crap, I can't believe she took off alone. She wouldn't know her way around and doesn't have a cell phone. It's not safe for her out there."

"How old is this girl?" Kade removed his Stetson and wiped his brow. "You're not heading for trouble, are you?"

Branch shot him a "keep out of it" look and rolled his shoulders. "Old enough but she is new to the US and in shock. We nearly died out there, and I promised to see her safely to her father. You know I don't break promises." He turned his glare on Gary. "I can't believe you just let her walk out of here."

"She is an adult, and I couldn't have prevented her leaving if I'd wanted to, but she didn't go alone. I made sure she caught the bus with others heading in the same direction. Like I said, she was booked on a flight out of Tampa." Gary opened his arms hands spread. "I don't recall you asking her to wait for you. I guess she decided leaving and avoiding the media was the best thing to do, you being a star and all." He rubbed the back of his neck. "You know the press will be all over the story of you alone with her in the hurricane. She could make a lot of money selling her side of things."

Gutted, he swallowed the lump in his throat then wiped the back of his hand across his cracked lips. Bone weary he sucked in a deep breath then let it whistle out between his teeth. "She isn't the type of girl to be impressed by fame, and I doubt she'll discuss anything that happened with a reporter." He had a sudden thought. "I have quite a few of her belongings in the saddlebags on my motorcycle. Did she leave a number for me to get in touch with her?"

"Can't say that she did." Gary cleared his throat and his cheeks pinked. "Seems to me she couldn't wait to get away."

What lies did you tell her about me? Forcing his mind to think straight, Branch nodded. The man was obviously hiding something, and there was not much point in attempting to push him for details. He wrinkled his nose at the smell in the room and tried another tack. He would need to cover his emotions or Gary would be telling all and sundry Susie had dumped him. "I'm not surprised she wanted to leave it's been a tough couple of days. At least I know she's okay." He indicated with his chin toward the door. I'll send someone to pick up the Indian. Thank you for your help." He offered Gary, his hand.

"It was a pleasure meeting you." Gary beamed at him.

With a heavy heart, Branch followed his brother out the building. Keeping his head low and ignoring the people badgering him for autographs who crowded around him like a hungry gaggle of geese, he made it to the chopper before Kade squeezed his shoulder.

"Hey, was this Susie someone special?" Kade threw open the chopper door and climbed into the seat. As Branch joined him, he gave him a look of brotherly concern. "Something is up with you or should I say 'down'. Since we got back, your mood is kind of blue and the last time you had an expression like that on your face was when our parents died."

"Susie was one special lady. Different from my usual girls. She was sweet but feisty, and I thought we had something going on between us." He shrugged not understanding why his heart hurt like a bitch. How had he misread her reaction toward him? He stared at his hands trying to understand where he'd gone wrong. "Seems I was mistaken."

CHAPTER NINE

The sun had set by the time the plane landed in Dallas and Susie sighed with relief at the sight of a woman in her thirties holding up a card with her name. Amelia Banks was dressed in an expensive navy business suit, cream silk blouse, and stilettos. She looked as if she had walked straight out of an executive's office. Susie glanced down at her grubby jeans and pushed back a lock of plane-tousled hair. "I'm Susie, thank you so much for coming, Amelia."

"You poor girl." Amelia patted her arm. "Come along now, my husband is driving around the block. The parking here is a nightmare." She led her to the exit. "What a horrible welcome to the US for you. Your father informed me you have lost everything."

And my heart too. Susie nodded. "Yes, I'm afraid so. I was lucky to escape with my life."

Outside the air-conditioned terminal, a wall of humidity hit her like a sledgehammer. The next moment a white car slid to a stop at the curb and Amelia pulled open the door for her. She climbed into the back seat and smiled at the handsome man behind the wheel. "Thank you so much for picking me up."

"Not a problem." He flicked a disinterested glance in her direction. "I'm Peter, and your father is a business associate. It was the least I could do."

The car sped away into the darkness, and the couple ignored her chatting between themselves as if she did not exist. Half an hour later, the car slid into a secure parking lot beneath a high-rise apartment building, and a metal roller door slid into place. Her attention moved over the expensive late model vehicles parked in neatly numbered slots. It would seem her father had married a woman of means. She opened the door and stepped out dragging her backpack behind her.

Amelia walked toward an elevator on her husband's arm, and she followed. Embarrassed by her shabby clothes and messy hair, she kept her distance.

"Oh yes." Amelia rummaged in her purse and pulled out a set of keys. "Here are the keys. You are on the top floor, the penthouse, and we are on the floor below. As your father would have informed you, the apartment was destined to go on the market next week. I have spent a considerable time overseeing the refurbishing. I hope you'll find the accommodation to your liking, if not, do let me know. We have already had quite a few offers. It is surprising how fast the news spreads when something so spectacular becomes available in this building."

Right now, Susie would be happy with a tent. Exhaustion and depression hit her in alternating waves. All she needed was a hot shower and sleep then she might be able to push the devastating thoughts of Branch Durham from her mind. She took the keys and nodded. "Thank you. I'm sure it will be wonderful."

The couple got out of the elevator without a backward glance, and the silver doors slid closed. The next time they opened, she stepped into a vestibule with thick royal blue carpet. Paintings of a city, she assumed was Dallas, decorated the walls each side of a set of impressive paneled double doors. She fumbled the set of keys but managed to open the door and stepped inside to complete darkness. Forcing her mind to overcome her phobia of the dark, she searched the wall for a switch. When light flooded the area, she gasped in surprise at the opulent surroundings. Marble floors, white leather furniture, and a flat-screen TV that took up most of one wall. A cool breeze drifted over her from the ducted air conditioning, and she laughed aloud. "This place is a fricking palace."

She explored moving from one dazzling room to the next. The kitchen could have supplied food for a small restaurant, and best of all Amelia had stocked the refrigerator with the essentials. She found coffee, and after staring at the contraption she recognized as one of those coffee machines that produced every style of coffee known to man, she had the beans ground and watched the first delicious drops fall into a bone china cup.

The bathroom, complete with the softest towels she had ever seen in her life and a selection of toiletries was her next port of call. The shower with jets that hit all the right places was heaven, and the soap made her skin feel pampered. She donned one of the bathrobes hanging behind the door, slipped on the matching slippers and headed back to the kitchen. Sitting at the island munching toast and drinking coffee should have been relaxing but Branch's face kept popping into her head. Why couldn't she stop thinking about him? He had not made any sort of commitment to her in their short time together. She had been a booty call, so why did her heart feel as if someone had crushed it underfoot?

She collected her toothbrush from her backpack, cleaned her teeth then strolled into the master bedroom. A huge bed dominated the room, and through the open blinds, the lights of Dallas twinkled like a million stars. She wanted to see her new home, but the soft pillows and clean sheets called to her. After sleeping rough, exhaustion took over, and the warm fuzzy feeling of sleep engulfed her.

The phone ringing woke her, and she opened her eyes to a blinding streak of sunlight. Sitting bolt upright she glanced around unaware of her surroundings. The persistent ringing came from the nightstand. She lifted the receiver. "Hello."

"Susan, this is your father. I'm calling to let you know, I've deposited five thousand dollars into your account. The car keys are on the bunch Amelia gave you. The vehicle is a silver Mercedes convertible. Get yourself some decent clothes and go to the beauty parlor. I have an image to maintain. Peter mentioned you looked like a bag lady."

Anger heated her cheeks. "I'm sure you would look a little disheveled if you'd been through a hurricane and been sleeping rough for days as well. I can't believe people could be so cruel to say such a thing."

"Well, you are in Dallas now, my dear, oil barons and the like. You'll need to up your game. I have to go. I'll call you in a few days. Do try and get a job."

The line went dead, and Susie stared at the receiver trying to process the conversation. Her impression of the locals had fallen, and if her life went any further down the toilet, she might just as well add a ticket back to the UK onto her shopping list. She slammed the receiver back in the cradle and stomped naked to the bathroom. "I just hope the shops are close by, I wouldn't want to contaminate the area."

* * * *

Branch spent the next few days trying to locate Susie. Well in truth, he had put his manager's entire office staff on the task of tracking down her father. However, finding a person newly arrived in a state was not easy. Her father had no phone number recorded, and as far as he could remember, the man was on his honeymoon. The initial search of the more popular hotels had not found him, and the remaining list was very long.

He had to put Susie out of his mind and concentrate on the rehearsals for his upcoming tour. In the morning, he would be on a flight to Nashville. The concert tour, spanning four months, and countless cities would leave him little time to sleep let alone worry if Susie was missing him. When he found her, and he *would* find her, no matter how long it took, he would attempt to rekindle the attraction between them. The sweet girl was a precious jewel, and he refused to give up on her. He rubbed the ache over his heart. The now familiar feeling of loss came whenever he thought about her. God help him, he had found his soul mate and let her slip through his fingers. Gutted, he stared down at his guitar and tried to concentrate on the next song. The drummer tapped a four-beat intro, and he turned toward the microphone, but the image of her sated after their lovemaking remained fixed in his mind. *I'm going to find you Susie and make you mine.*

The songs of heartbreak and finding that special girl suddenly had a new meaning and four months later when he took the stage at the final concert of the tour, his need to find the girl of his dreams had become an obsession. The audience cheered as he played the introduction to a new song. Wanting to explain the lyrics to his fans, he lifted a hand to stop the band and leaned into the microphone.

"I wrote, 'The Girl I Left Behind', for a special lady." He scanned the eager faces staring up at him and smiled. "During the hurricane, I found a beautiful mermaid on the beach. She must have been a Siren as the moment I heard her voice, she captured my heart." He pounded his chest with one fist. "But like the elusive mythical creature, when I returned she'd vanished and although I've searched for her, it's as if I imagined her." He strummed a note on his guitar and stared into the camera beaming the live feed across the nation. "This one is for you, sweet mermaid. If you're out there, I sure need you to contact my manager, Dirk Ford at Brightway Entertainment."

He repeated the same message at the close of every performance in the last two months. Under a single spotlight, he stood alone, just a man and his guitar. The audience fell silent, and he poured out his heart, using his music to convey his feelings. His voice filled the arena, a lonely cowboy telling the world about the girl he loved then lost. In the front row, he caught sight of tears glistening on the cheeks of the girls, and the men's faces bore his pain. The song would be a hit but he no longer cared and when he hit the last note, the audience exploded into applause. Emotionally drained, he left the stage without returning for an encore.

In the wings, he passed his guitar to the roadie who dutifully placed it in its case and handed it to Dirk, his manager. The guitar went with him everywhere. He followed the lights down the back steps and forced his mouth into a smile. The fans with backstage passes pressed against the aluminum barriers lining his walkway. After mopping the sweat from his face, he paused to sign autographs, his gaze drifting over the women's faces hoping Susie had found him. He had seen her, or rather *thought* he'd seen her many times only to discover his mistake. One of the backup band elbowed him in the ribs and leaned in to speak to him. He stepped away from the reaching hands and turned to him. "Yeah, Dean, what's up?"

"See anything you like? I'm inviting a few girls back to the hotel."

The end of tour party was a recurring event, and yeah, he had indulged in the past, but since meeting Susie, his appetite for groupies had waned. Singing was his passion and performing his music in front of adoring fans had once been all he needed, but the spark had gone out of his life. He shook his head. "You do whatever you like, but I'm taking the first flight back to Dallas. I have some private business to attend to." He turned back to his fans to dutifully sign autographs and pose for selfies.

When Dirk pulled him away and dragged him toward the exit, he sighed with relief. "Thanks, man, I'm beat."

In the backseat of the limousine, he turned to his manager. "Now the tour is over, I'm going to Hawaii to look for Susie."

"Have you lost your ever-loving mind? You will not be able to find her without help. People come and go all the time in Hawaii. She might have left the country. You said she wasn't close to her father, and the hurricane finished her career. I would bet she returned home to her mom. It's what most young girls would do in the same situation."

"She is not a quitter." Branch shook his head in denial. "We had something special going on, and I reckon the guy at the shelter, Gary someone, got in her ear about me and scared her off." He rubbed the back of his neck. "It's the only explanation for her to hightail it out of my life without as much as a goodbye."

Dirk's brow crinkled into a frown. "I know what's going on with you, Branch. Usually, women throw themselves at you, and this one walked away. It's obvious you're suffering from a type of rejection syndrome or something." He snorted. "Holy shit, man, you don't even *know* for sure she went to Hawaii, do you?"

Branch wiped sweat from his face with the towel Dirk handed him then shook his head. "Nope, I know she called her father in Hawaii. I assumed she went to be with him, but I really have no idea." He stared at Dirk and blinked as a thought filtered into his mind. "Holy cow, I've remembered something. She called her father from the shelter because she didn't have a cell phone. The shelters take down the details of the people who stay with them and would have her father's phone number as a next of kin contact. If he was on his honeymoon, likely she had his cell phone number."

"Yeah, true enough but there is no way in hell they'll give out that information." Dirk rubbed his chin looking surreal as they sped along the highway and the streetlights flashed over him making his image like an old home movie. "Unless . . . you said Susie was English, right?"

"Yeah, well no." Branch shrugged. "She sounds English, but she was born in Boston."

"I have an English secretary working in my office, Jenny Weeks. She is a temp, filling in after Jane won that trip to Las Vegas. She is from the agency I use when the office staff are on vacation, but I'm sure if I throw her a few bucks, she will help. If she calls the shelter looking for Susie as a concerned friend from the UK. A woman might be able to persuade the official to hand out Susie's information." Dirk grinned. "Or at least, she can ask them to pass a phone number to her father. I'm sure they would do that, and he is likely to call and give Susie her number. You did mention they aren't close, so he is not going to know her friends, is he? What do you think?"

"Yeah, but Susie will know it's not a friend, won't she? Maybe get her to say she is a friend of her stepfather. Neither of them will know *his* friends. We'll give them my cell phone number and hope at least one of them calls." Branch leaned back in the seat and for the first time in ages, the pain in his heart eased.

CHAPTER TEN

Life in Dallas was interesting, to say the least. Within one week of arriving, Susie had secured a position as the assistant manager of North Fort, a prestigious hotel four blocks from her apartment building. The people there treated her with respect, which was more than she could say for some of the oil baron patrons. Although many gave her outrageously high tips, others treated her like dirt. Some complained about her British accent, saying they could not understand a word she uttered and refused to have anything to do with her. Of course, this attitude made her life a misery because it was company policy for the assistant manager to escort the more wealthy clients to their rooms. Ignoring any rudeness with a fixed smile, she made sure she catered for their every whim with a smile.

The job aside, she had bigger problems to keep her awake at night. She tried in vain to push Branch from her mind, but the media splashed him over the news and internet in a constant reminder on a weekly basis. His music played on every damn radio station and worst of all over the speakers at work. Now she had a constant reminder of their time together, and her secret was growing at an alarming rate. At first, she refused to believe she could possibly be pregnant blaming missing her monthly on the stress of going through a hurricane. After all, she had not suffered morning sickness and put the tiredness down to the new job. Four months later, her breasts had increased in size, and her nipples had become supersensitive. Not long after the possibility had sunk into her bewildered brain, a home pregnancy test had confirmed her fears.

I am carrying a megastar's baby.

Sitting in front of her laptop, she drew a deep breath then typed Branch's name in the search engine. She guessed it was time to find out more about the father of her child although, she had decided not to inform him. The reasons had made her decision easy. She was fifty percent sure Branch had used protection each time they had made love, and he would not believe the baby was his. In fact, he would more likely decide she was a fortune hunter and have his attorney deal with her to shut her up. After all, they had been through, a man who could not be bothered to say goodbye to her would not be happy discovering he had fathered a child with a woman he hardly knew. No, it would be better to carry on alone. She had health insurance to cover the birth, and her next concern would be to make sure she could support her baby. After applying to companies with vacant positions for accountants working from home, she had secured a trial position. If the company liked her work, she would be self-sufficient, especially as her father had transferred the title of the apartment and Daphne's car into her name. If everything fell into place, her future looked secure. She would have the baby of the man she adored and would give Branch's child all her love and devotion. *I'll be okay.*

As Branch's image filled the laptop screen, she bit down hard on the inside of her cheek. He was so handsome, her skin prickled with goose bumps at the memory of his mouth on her tender breasts, and the way he stroked her, licked her, kissed her. She groaned wanting to turn away and forget him, but then she noticed the headlines over a video file. *Branch makes a plea to find his elusive mermaid.*

With shaking fingers, she hit the play button, and the screen came to life. Branch sat center stage in a single spotlight. His deep hypnotic voice filled the room with a song straight from his heart. When he stared into the camera as if singing to her, his words of lost love registered in her mind and tears welled up in her eyes. *Oh, my God, he is singing about me.*

When the applause died down, and he pleaded for his mermaid to contact his manager, she gaped at the screen. Heart pounding, she replayed the song several times allowing tears to stream down her cheeks. She touched the screen running her fingers over his face remembering every contour and line. The idea he had searched for her, *was* searching for her, made her heart race with excitement, but would he still want her now? Indecision fell over her like a shroud. She needed time to think of the consequences before contacting him. The idea of him rejecting her again would be too much to bear. He would require proof at least of how far her pregnancy had progressed. First, she would make an appointment with an obstetrician and then she needed to talk to her mother.

* * * *

Branch paced up and down Dirk's office, his gaze not moving from the woman sitting at the front desk. "Why hasn't he called back yet?"

"The person in the shelter said Gary wouldn't be back until after two." Dirk glanced at the clock on the wall. "It's five after, give him a bit longer."

"First the man goes on vacation, and now he is permanently out to lunch. I'll take the chopper and go see him personally before long and shake the damn phone number out of him." Branch stopped pacing and stared with anticipation at Dirk's secretary. "She is making the call. He has to be there this time."

Five minutes later, the woman got up from her seat and with a slip of paper in one hand sashayed into the office smiling at him.

"I have the number you require, Mr. Durham. Gary was very nice and gave me Mr. Blake's cell phone number." She waved the paper in front of him. "Anything else I can do for you?"

Branch ignored the suggestive sweep of the tip of her tongue across her red lips and nodded. "Yeah, I want *you* to call the number. Tell Mr. Blake you are a friend of Susie's stepfather from the UK and you heard about the hurricane and wanted to find out if she is okay. Ask where you can contact her because you intend to come to the US for a holiday soon and would like to meet up with her."

"You want me to *lie* for you, Mr. Durham?" She pouted and pushed out one hip in a show of indignation. "I'm not sure if I can do that for you."

Branch reached for the billfold in his back pocket and counted five one-hundred-dollar bills from the wad of cash. He dropped it on Dirk's desk and raised a brow. "Will this help your conscience?"

"I'm sure I could bend the rules one time."

When she went to snatch the notes, Branch covered the money with his hand. He met her gaze and noticed the come-on look had vanished. "Make the call then you can have the cash and use Dirk's phone. I want to hear every word."

"Very well." She reached for the phone and punched in the number. "Mr. Blake, this is Vicky Wills, I'm a friend of Susie's stepfather. He gave me your number when I left the UK and said you would be able to put me in touch with her." Vicky took a pen from a holder on Dirk's desk and tapped it on the pad. "Oh, yes I heard about the hurricane. I had no idea she was in Florida at the time. How awful, well I'm sure she'll be glad to hear from a family friend." She jotted down a phone number then an address. "How wonderful, I had planned to visit Dallas on my trip. Thank you so much. Bye." She placed the phone back in the receiver and lifted her gaze to Branch. "It would seem Susie has been in Dallas since she left the shelter." She ripped the note from the pad and handed it to him. "Swank address too. Is that all?"

Branch swallowed the lump in his throat and nodded then glanced down at the familiar address. His heart pounded in his chest, and suddenly he had no idea what to do next. He lifted his gaze to Dirk. "One-half of me wants to drive there straight away the other half wants me to call her first to make sure she wants to see me." He dashed a hand through his hair. "Darn, I'll go home and make myself presentable, buy flowers, then just show up on her doorstep and ask her out to dinner."

"It's been a while, maybe she has a boyfriend." Dirk glanced away not meeting his eyes and cleared his throat. "Your plea for her to contact you has been on social media, TV, and the press. If she'd wanted to see you, she would have found you by now."

"You don't know Susie." Branch rubbed his chin. "She isn't the type to go chasing a guy. I'm guessing she expects me to find her and the idea of her finding another man — no way. What we had was special in ways I wouldn't expect you to understand." *I was her first.*

"Then go all caveman and claim your woman." Dirk waved him from the office. "But keep it low-key, the media will be all over your reunion, and if she is as shy as you say, the moment they get involved, the honeymoon will be well and truly over."

Elation mixed with a strange fear bubbled inside him. Dirk was correct, low-key would be the best way to handle the situation. He would recreate their first time together sans the hurricane and have a picnic basket made up. Glancing at the address, he frowned wondering how Susie could afford to live in a penthouse apartment in that area. The idea she might have met a wealthy oil baron's son flitted across his mind and made his stomach cramp. He straightened, pushed his Stetson down over his eyes and stepped into the elevator. She was his soulmate dammit and no man, no matter how rich, was going to cut his grass. Whatever had happened to her since she vanished from his life did not matter, and he would insist they at least talk. He needed to hold her again and tell her how much he cared for her — boyfriend be damned.

* * * *

Exhausted after a long day on her feet, Susie parked her car then took the elevator to her apartment. Sighing with relief, she kicked off her shoes, dumped her bag on the nearest chair, and practically fell into the bathroom. A long, hot shower had been calling her name for hours. Her feet ached, her back ached, in fact, every muscle in her body ached. The elevator had broken down at the hotel, and the manager expected her to haul the guest's bags up the stairs. With people arriving for the weekend, she had climbed the stairs numerous times in the past three hours to escort annoyed patrons to their rooms. *Thank God, I've finished working with those awful people.*

She stripped dropping her clothes into the laundry hamper then stepping into the luxurious shower cubicle. For some time, she stood leaning against the tile allowing the water to massage her tired flesh. Her stomach rumbled reminding her lunch had been six hours ago and she tinkered with the idea of ordering a pizza or Chinese takeout. Although, she usually made the effort to cook a healthy dinner or even a cold meat salad for the best nutrition, being exhausted was not good during pregnancy either. She pressed one hand on her stomach and smiled into the steam. Not being the skinny model type had been an advantage after all, she could hide her growing bump for at least another month, and most would believe she had gained a few pounds. She survived the last week in her job, and how she looked would no longer matter. She had finished rinsing the conditioner from her hair when she heard the door chimes. Reluctantly, she turned off the water, wrapped a large bath towel around her body, another covered her hair and tiptoed over the expensive pure wool carpet to the intercom. "Yes?"

"I have a delivery for Miss Blake."

"Put it in the lift and press the button for the penthouse." She would need to put on a dressing gown before she ventured into the hall and turned away.

An annoyed male voice crackled through the intercom.

"I'll need a signature, Miss Blake. You wouldn't want me to lose my job now would you?"

Susie stared at the speaker not sure what to do. She sucked in a deep breath. No doubt, this was the first batch of ledgers from her new employer. "Is the package from Baxter's?"

"*Yes, ma'am.*"

"Come on up."

She ran into the bathroom, grasped her bathrobe, and wrapped it tightly around her, then dragged a hairbrush through her wet hair. When the knock came at her door, she peered through the peephole but could only make out a man's Adam's apple. Whoever was at her door must be tall. She cranked open the door and peered through the crack. A wide white smile she knew so well greeted her. *Branch.*

"Hello, darlin'." Branch held up a large basket then placed one hand on the door. "Can I come inside? I think we need to talk."

CHAPTER ELEVEN

Susie stared at Branch in disbelief. Her tall, dark, and gorgeous cowboy met her gaze with a sexy wink. As if he had walked out of one of her dreams, he stood on her doorstep looking so amazingly handsome she lost the power of speech. Unable to process the vision before her, she inhaled a scent as familiar as breathing. Some moments passed before she gathered her wits and stood to one side. Without caring about the consequences, she allowed him to enter. "You are the last person I ever thought I'd see standing on my doorstep."

"Why?" Branch placed the basket on the floor and moved closer. He cupped the back of her neck in one large hand sending a trail of goose bumps down her spine. "I've been looking for you for months, and here you are living in Dallas right under my nose." He nuzzled her ear. "Why is it you are soaking wet when I find you? I'm beginning to believe you really are a mermaid. Mmm, did I mention, you smell delicious?"

"I just got out the shower."

"So I can see." He suckled her earlobe then chuckled. "Seeing you like this brings back wonderful memories of the day we met."

She pulled back and stared at him. "When a hurricane almost killed us, you mean?"

"Nope, when I held you in my arms for the first time, and we made spectacular love as if it was the end of the world." A shadow of doubt crossed his features. "Although, I must be a lousy lover for you to leave me. I guess I'll have to try harder in the future."

All resentment toward him faded at his sincere expression. He had after all tried to find her and she had avoided his plea to contact his manager. *We are both to blame.* Susie shook her head then giggled. "You are a wonderful lover — not that I have anyone else to rate you against."

"Mmm, well that's a good thing." He nibbled along her chin. "Hush now, we'll discuss why you ran away from me later . . . much later."

The delicious scent of him filled her nostrils, and the heat from him radiated through the thin bathrobe awakening her desire and peaking her nipples. She lifted her chin intending to remind him he walked out on her and not the other way around but didn't get the chance. His soft mouth came down in a warm caress teasing her to open for him. All doubts vanished the moment their lips met. He was here. Her big, strong, cowboy and she wanted him. She moaned and threw her arms around his neck, kissing him back with fervor. He slid his warm hands inside the bathrobe, eased the garment from her shoulders then scooped her naked into his strong arms and smiled.

"Bedroom?"

Overcome with lust for the man of her dreams, Susie waved a hand toward the hallway. When he chuckled and strode into her bedroom, she came to her senses. "Wait, I need to tell you something."

"Unless you want me to leave, we can talk later." Branch laid her on the bed and pulled back the sheets. He pushed her onto the pillows and gazed down at her with passion. "I need you, darlin', and by the way your nipples have risen to greet me, I *know* you want me." He sat beside her and bent to lick one straining bud. "You take my breath away. I've missed you so much. Please don't send me away, Susie."

The way he looked at her, he made her feel beautiful. Under his gaze, she became a goddess and left the unsure girl embarrassed by her figure far behind. She opened her arms, and he went to her, devouring her mouth, his tongue scraping every erogenous zone. When finally he lifted his head, he met her gaze and smiled.

"Take off my shirt. I want you to touch me." He chuckled at her struggles then dragged the offending garment over his head.

Next, he kicked off his boots then stood to empty his pockets onto the nightstand before peeling off his jeans.

Her attention moved over his remarkable body, from his wide shoulders and broad chest, down to his massive erection. When he went for the condoms in his jean's pocket, she stilled his arm. "You don't need to use a condom, and I want to feel you inside me."

"I haven't been with another woman since our time together." Branch flicked a glance at her, his expression hidden by long black lashes. "And I usually don't risk having sex without protection — are you sure it's okay?"

Susie ran her hand up his thigh, glorying at the flesh beneath her palm. "Yes, I'm *very* sure, and by the way, I haven't had sex with anyone else either."

"I'm glad you waited for me." He slid over her kissing his way up her belly to suckle her tender nipples.

She arched pushing her breasts toward him. "I've been dreaming about you making love to me."

"Me too." He kissed a sizzling path down her chest licked her navel then slid between her thighs.

When his tongue probed her folds, found her hard nub, and circled, she cried out in ecstasy. He held her hips in his warm hands and ravished her, driving her higher with every tormenting swirl of his hot tongue. She gripped handfuls of the sheet and tossed her head. "Please, Branch. Oh God, it's too much."

The wonderful sensation curled deep in her belly and exploded in a rush leaving her floating somewhere in erotic space. The next moment he was inside her, thick and hot. His mouth closed on her breast, and his hips rolled taking her back up again on a slow sensual ride. She lifted her legs and gripped his hips, tilting her bottom. Ripples of delight surged inside her with every deep plunge, and she grasped his shoulders pulling him down to her. He moaned and kissed her deeply and with one hard shove pushed her over the edge in a shattering orgasm. She clung to him limbs trembling and overcome by emotion tears filled her eyes. She blinked them away but not quick enough for him to notice.

"I've hurt you." He eased up on his elbows and stared down at her with a tragic expression. "Darn it, Susie, you should have stopped me."

She cupped his face and smiled at him. "No, you didn't hurt me. It was beautiful. I'm so happy you found me." The memory of being pregnant slapped her in the face, and she frowned. "But we should have talked before we made love, Branch."

"I couldn't wait, and nothing was more important than showing you how much I've missed you." He ran the tip of his finger over her wet cheek. "I get worried when you cry. Women confuse me when they cry because they're happy." He eased away from her, then rolled onto one side and gave her a lopsided smile. "I couldn't think of anything more important than making love to you, but we *do* need to talk. Ladies first."

Gathering her courage, Susie lifted her chin. "Prepare yourself for a shock and don't hate me, okay?"

"Why would I ever hate you, darlin'?"

Heart thundering, she met his intelligent gaze. He had found her, said he cared for her, but she would not be able to hide her pregnancy from him for long. It would be better to tell him and then see if he wanted her. Sucking in a deep breath, she counted to three in her head.

"I'm pregnant."

Branch thought he had misheard her and shook his head. "What?"

"I'm pregnant." Susie slid off the bed snatched up her bathrobe and pulled it on with jerking movements. "It's okay. I don't expect you to *do* anything. To be honest, that is the reason why I haven't contacted you. I'm sure you have women trying to thrust babies on you all the time, but I wouldn't do something so awful to you, Branch. Don't worry, I'll be just fine managing on my own, but if you plan on dropping by again, I thought you should know."

He pushed both hands through his hair. She did say she hadn't been with another man and now she claimed to be pregnant. It could not possibly be his baby. Jesus, it had been almost five months since they last slept together and he had used protection. He examined her from top to toe, and apart from glowing from obvious good health, or great sex, she sure didn't look pregnant. "How far along are you?"

"I'm about eighteen weeks gone. I'll get a lot bigger very fast from now on, I'm afraid." She wet her lips, and her voice dropped to just below a whisper. "You are the father, Branch. Do you believe me?"

Dumbstruck, he gaped at her not certain if he should run for the hills or stay and listen to her story. The idea of him being the father was ludicrous. The situation was fast becoming one his manager had warned him about and the last thing he expected from Susie. "I'm having trouble getting my head around this, darlin'. Careful is my middle name. You know that, right?"

"Well, yes. I thought you used protection, but nothing is one hundred percent effective." She shrugged. "It was a shock for me too you know. I'm not sure how I'm going to explain this to my father. He has been very kind to me, gave me a car, and this apartment as compensation for losing two year's work as his manager. I've been working as an assistant manager of a hotel but have found a job working from home, so you need not be involved unless you want to?"

The implications of what she said swirled around his brain. He stared at her beautiful face not knowing what to say. He cleared his throat. "Are you sure? Have you taken a test?"

"Of course I have, silly, and I've seen a gynecologist. Give me your hand." Susie moved closer and pressed his palm against her belly. "See it's not fat, it's rounded and hard. My boobs are bigger too, didn't you notice?"

He moved his hand with gentle care over the rounded bump and swallowed hard. Her beautiful breasts had filled his hands, and he had noticed her nipples were a deeper shade. "Okay, so I agree you're pregnant, but it's been a long time since we made love, Susie, if this baby is mine, you should be out here by now." He made a round curve with his hand over her belly. "Small doesn't run in our family. All us Durham boys weighed in at nine pounds and over at birth."

"Fine, it's obvious you don't believe me. Thanks for dropping by but now it's time for you to go." Her bottom lip trembled. "Go back to your ranch and forget I ever told you, it will be better that way."

"I'm *not* leaving you again, Susie." He chewed on his bottom lip. "It's not that I don't believe you, it is a shock is all."

"Why? I haven't asked you to be involved or to take responsibility." She threw up her hands. "I just knew you'd act like this. Hell, Branch, you look like a trapped animal. Go — get out of here. I don't *need* you. I am quite capable of managing on my own — I don't need a man in my life."

Branch swallowed the lump in his throat. His brain refused to think straight. "Holy cow, you didn't *want* me to know? Why the hell, not, Susie?"

"I didn't want to ruin my memory of you, Branch. Now you've spoiled everything." She let out a small sob and covered her mouth. "*Please* go now."

The sight of her distress broke his heart. "You must think I'm some kind of an asshole if you believe I would walk out on what's mine and leave a kid without a daddy. Remember, I know what that's like. I'm not that kind of guy, and I'm not going anywhere until we sort out a few things."

"Fine. Do you need proof I'm pregnant and how many weeks? I'm sure you can count." Susie moved stiffly toward the nightstand and took an envelope out of her purse.

He rubbed his chin remembering the one time during the hurricane he had made love to her without protection, but it had been a once only. He looked up at her forlorn face, and his heart twisted. He *loved* her and nothing would change his deep feelings toward her. In fact, even if the baby turned out not to be his, he would take care of her. He did not intend to lose her again. "Come here and sit by me." He held out a hand to her. "What do you have there?"

"Baby photos." She sat beside him on the bed and handed him a film negative. "There is a written report from the doctor here as well confirming the duration of my pregnancy."

Only a fool would question the specialist's report. The time worked out. Holy shit, it *was* his baby. A strange euphoria swirled inside him. *I'm going to be a daddy.* Pushing down the urge to pick Susie up and swing her around with joy he turned on the bedside lamp and held the strange image up to the light. He could not make head or tail of the picture and turned to her. "Okay, I believe you, the baby is mine, but it's hard to see what this is. It looks like two halves of a snail shell."

"Silly." Susie pointed to the strange outline. "Here is the head, and the backbone, and that dark bit is the heart. On the scan, I could see it pumping away. In a couple of weeks, I will find out the sex."

He turned the image around and stared at a replica of the exact same thing she had shown him. He raised a brow. "Why does it look like an upside-down mirror image?"

Susie stared at the document in her hand then shrugged.

"Susie." Branch lifted her chin with one finger and gazed into her worried blue eyes. "What is it? Is something wrong with the baby?"

"No, nothing is *wrong*. I'm having twins." She laid a protective hand over her belly and lifted a sorrowful gaze to him. "I'm so sorry."

Twins? The shock subsided, replaced by a wave of elation and he whooped with joy then pulled her into his arms. "Twins?" He pulled back and stared down at her grinning. "We are having *twins*. Darlin', you have made me the happiest man alive."

Susie buried her face in his chest and allowed the tears to fall. When he held her close, stroking her hair and murmuring endearments in her ear, she lifted her head to look at him. In the dim light, she could not make out his expression, but his touch said everything she needed to know. His kiss was tender and words reassuring. With each of his intimate caresses, she pushed away her worries and melted against him. When he made love to her, slowly with deep passion, she orgasmed calling out his name. In one evening together, the time they spent apart seemed to vanish into an unpleasant memory. Branch had found her.

Sometime later, she lifted her head and looked at him. The sight of him, hair tousled and his eyes half shut made her toes curl with delight. She ran her palm over his muscular chest and circled one flat nipple. When he mirrored her actions, she sighed in delight. "You make me feel so good."

"Uh-huh. You make me feel . . . ah . . . like a bear at a honeypot. I can't get enough of you, darlin'." He rested a hand on her belly and met her gaze, his expression turned serious. "I'm not looking forward to telling my grandma." He frowned and chewed on his bottom lip. "She raised us right and getting you pregnant is irresponsible."

A shiver of worry spilled down her spine. "I would think the first thing she would worry about is if you are really the father."

"I would say that would be her first question." He gathered her against his broad chest, and she could hear his heart beating. "I'll show her the picture, she'll be over the moon you're having twins."

"You don't have to tell her right away." Susie snuggled into his arms. "Because I'm carrying twins I can arrange a very safe paternity test. I don't want you or your family to have any doubts. I'll set it up for Monday. Will you come to the doctors with me they will need a sample from you?"

"Sure, but I don't need any proof. I can feel it inside every time I touch you." His stomach growled, and he looked at her apologetically. "Darlin', I'm hungry enough to eat a horse, and there is a picnic basket out there calling my name."

She sat away from him and smiled. "I'm famished, and I'm eating for three now. I'll make a pot of coffee if you bring the basket to the kitchen. You don't mind eating in there, do you?"

"No, that's fine." He brushed a kiss over her lips. "Take a shower with me first. I'll get the basket unloaded while you dry your hair. I don't want you getting a chill."

"I love the way you take care of me, but you go first. I'm sure if we get in the shower together we'll have little chance of making it to the kitchen." Susie pressed a warm kiss to his mouth and stroked his thigh. "I'm crazy about you, Branch, and can't get enough of you."

"Lord, woman, if you keep this up, I won't make it to the shower."

CHAPTER TWELVE

By the end of the meal, Branch had Susie giggling as he told her stories of the crazy things that went wrong during his tour. "One night, I went back to my hotel room and not two minutes after I stepped in the shower, six girls clad only in their underwear came rushing in." He refilled his coffee mug and grinned. "I hung onto that cubicle door so tight I thought my fingers would break, then I said to them. 'Even I haven't enough energy to make love to all of you at once. You all go outside and wait in the hall, and I'll call you in two at a time.' Well, darlin', they all nodded and left the room." He grinned at Susie's wide-eyed expression. "I locked the door and called security. Dang, I'd swear a couple of them were under eighteen, and I have no idea who they paid off to access my room."

"Does that happen a lot?" Susie took a chocolate from the large box on the table and popped it into her mouth with a sigh leaving a smear of chocolate on her bottom lip.

He wanted to lick the candy from her mouth and cleared his throat. "The women trying to get laid, yeah, I'm afraid so. It's part of the job." He chuckled at her hurt expression. "I don't sleep with them, darlin'." He touched her hand and squeezed. "I have once or twice in the past but not now and no one at all since I met you. Why didn't you call me? You know, when you left the shelter."

"I didn't have your number." Susie took a cell phone from the bench and placed it on the table. "I didn't have a phone, if you remember?" She pushed a strand of blonde hair behind one ear. "Not that I tried to find you. I thought our brief affair was over."

He could feel her drifting away from him. The hurt in her eyes radiated through him cramping his gut. *She doesn't trust me anymore.* He took her phone and added his number then rang his cell. "There, now I have your number as well. I made a mistake, I should have given you my number, but it slipped my mind at the time. All I could think about was the Smithers all alone with a gang of thugs bearing down on them, and I thought you'd wait for me at the shelter."

"*I thought* when you said *your people* would arrange for me to go to my father it was your way of leaving without creating a scene." A frown creased her brow. "The man in charge of the shelter, Gary, said you were a player and wouldn't be coming back."

Holy shit! I'd like to get my hands on that asshole. "He knows nothing about me, darlin', and after being with me, you must have known I cared about you. I told you as much." He gazed into her concerned eyes wanting to take away the pain he had caused her. "Can I stay with you tonight?"

"Why?" Susie pulled her hand away and tossed back a lock of silken hair from her face.

He noticed her fingers tremble and wanted to hold her. "I want to cuddle you, make love to you. I want to convince you I'm not planning to run out on you. I'm hoping I'll be able to persuade you to stay the weekend with me at my ranch. One evening isn't long enough to make plans for our future."

"I would like to see your ranch, but I'm not ready to meet your family. Seeing you again is more than I can handle right now." She nibbled on her fingertips and dropped her gaze to the table. "Once they find out about the babies, they'll think I'm after your money, and probably believe I set you up."

His brother Hunter would take a lot of convincing. Branch winced. "My family will listen to me." He cleared his throat. "They all know I've been searching for you, darlin', but you don't have to worry, I don't live with them. Don't you remember me telling you I have my own place?"

"Yes, I remember the stories about the ranch." She lifted her troubled blue gaze. "It sounded like paradise."

"It is." He smiled and covered her hand. "Private with fantastic views, a huge swimming pool, and did I say 'private'?"

"You did." Susie wet her lips in a slow seductive move. "Are you sure, Branch, *really* sure you want to be with me? I don't want you to feel obligated because of one mistake. I couldn't stand you feeling sorry for me."

He gave her a quick hard look and shook his head slowly. "Darlin', did the way I made love to you seem like an obligation?" He snorted. "Because if you have any doubts about how I feel about you — and our babies, I'm sure I can change your mind, real fast."

Relieved, Susie could not stop grinning. "I think I might have a few doubts." She giggled. "Maybe quite a few. Our discussion could last all night."

"You'll be the death of me." Branch chuckled and pushed to his feet. "I'll need to go downstairs I left my overnight bag in the car."

She flicked her hair over one shoulder and laughed. "Oh, so you had this all planned, did you?"

Branch's sensuous mouth lifted at the corner.

"I hoped you'd at least talk to me, but no I hadn't planned to stay. I usually have an overnight bag in my car. With the paparazzi hounding me I often have to take refuge in a hotel." He headed for the door. "I'm parked not far from the building. I'll be back in five."

Susie collected her spare set of house keys from the kitchen drawer. "Here, point this toggle at the gate and park in my bay, I have three. They all have 'penthouse' written on them. I don't want you to get mobbed if anyone sees you wandering the streets alone." She handed him the keys. "I'll clean up here."

"Thanks." He moved toward her and brushed a kiss over one cheek. "You smell so good. I want to lick you all over."

"Then hurry back." She pushed him on the shoulder. "I'll be waiting."

Branch pushed the keys into his pocket and headed for the elevator. Once inside, he called his brother, Kade. "I've found her. Yeah, Dirk managed to track her down in Dallas. I'm bringing her back to the ranch for the weekend so keep everyone clear. I'll talk later." He shut the phone not wanting to make excuses or explanations.

Making his way outside the main doors of the apartment building, he headed for the Mustang parked in the shadows under a tree. He could slip along the shady sidewalk unnoticed and be inside the parking lot in a few minutes. As he approached his car, the door to a van parked further down the street slid open, and a woman staggered out, tripped then fell to her knees. Branch swore under his breath, strode past his car, and went to offer assistance. "Are you okay, ma'am?" He bent forward and offered his hand. Although the woman avoided his gaze, she seemed vaguely familiar, but he could not place her. He touched her shoulder. "Are you ill? Do you want me to call nine-one-one?"

The next moment, pain shot through his head, and he stumbled falling against the van. His vision blurred but his survival instinct remained intact. His father often said he had a thick skull and after surviving three years on the rodeo circuit before he reached twenty-one, it would take more than one blow to the head to floor him. In two steps, he regained his balance and swung around fists raised. "What the hell?"

The fuzzy images of two men wavered before him their faces obscured by balaclavas. If they planned to mug him they would be out of luck, his wallet was on the nightstand in Susie's bedroom. If they wanted his car, he sure as hell would not be giving it up without a fight, not after waiting four long months to get the vehicle shipped back and restored. He brushed at the trickle of blood running down his face and snorted. Two street punks he could take down with one hand tied behind his back, especially as one looked as if he spent his life eating doughnuts. He blinked to clear his vision then took a step backward at the sight of two Glock 22's pointing at his chest.

His heart rate went into overdrive and his attention pinned on the guns. The men appeared too casual as if rather than a random mugging they had planned his abduction. Holy shit, if this was someone's idea of a joke, there would be hell to pay. Having little choice, he raised both hands. "What do you want?"

"Hands behind your back, nice and easy." The fat guy waved his pistol toward Branch's head. "Do as we say and all this will be over real soon."

"What will be over?" Branch flicked his gaze in all directions, but the street was deserted. He squared his shoulders. "I don't have any money on me. You can search me if you like." He lifted his chin. "Let me go, and I'll forget this ever happened."

"Nope, you're coming with us for a little ride." Fat Guy's finger moved onto the trigger sending an ice-cold shard of fear ricocheting down Branch's spine. "Get into the van."

"I'm not going anywhere with you." Branch glared at him. "It would be in your best interest if you walked away."

"Think you're special, huh? Well to me you're just a well-paid job." Fat Guy gave a low chuckle and moved closer bringing with him the stink of sweat. "I suggest you do as I say because it makes no difference if you arrive at your next destination with just the bump on your head or with both kneecaps smashed. Your choice."

Out of the corner of his eye, he noticed a third man swinging a baseball bat in one hand. No doubt the one who had hit him from behind. As good a brawler he might be, he would have little chance against three armed men, plus the woman who had conveniently moved out of his line of sight. He rubbed his chin praying for someone, anyone, to drive by so he could raise the alarm. They had proved they had no problem injuring him and by the amount of blood running down his cheek, he needed a few stitches. If he resisted they would incapacitate him and drag him away, but if he cooperated, he would be fit enough to escape. As if conceding defeat, he nodded. "Okay, I'll go with you but will you at least tell me *why* you're kidnapping me?" He put both hands behind his back.

"I don't have to tell you anything, but I will say if you do as you're told you'll live." Fat Guy pushed the muzzle of the Glock so hard into his cheek it ground against his teeth. "I'd sure like to mess up your pretty face and one punch into your larynx would sure as hell finish your career. Think about that before you give me or my boys a reason to play with you some."

They had recognized him. His mind reeled with the implications. Did they intend to hold him for ransom? *Holy shit,* that plot usually ended up with someone dead in the movies. How had they found him? Only three people had Susie's address and knew his plans to leave his bodyguard behind when visiting her this evening. One was his brother, Kade, so that left Dirk, and the new English secretary, Jenny Weeks. His mind went to the woman he offered to assist and the penny dropped. *Jenny Weeks.* He had become the target of a well-organized plan. The Weeks woman had taken the temporary position at Dirk's office after his secretary, Jane, had conveniently won a trip. Yeah, Miss Weeks's job was to discover his movements with the intention of kidnapping him to extract money from his family. All they had to do was wait for him to leave Susie's apartment to catch him alone. He had not divulged his intention to stay overnight to anyone because he had not known if Susie would welcome him or kick him to the curb. *Susie. Dang, she'll think I've walked out on her again.*

The plastic zip ties cut deep into his flesh tightening with a ripping sound then a smelly dark cloth bag fell over his head. He gagged as the odor of rotten fish burned his nostrils and slammed his mouth shut. Pushed forward, his knees collided painfully with the opening of the van. He refused to cry out and did not resist the hands rolling him onto a hard metal floor. As the others climbed inside, the van rocked then took off slowly before accelerating in what he believed was a southerly direction. As the vehicle swerved around corners, throwing him about the floor, nausea gripped him. "Do you mind if I sit up?"

He heard a grunt to his left. Agony speared white flashes in his eyes, and everything went black.

CHAPTER THIRTEEN

After hours passed and Branch had not returned, despair followed the excitement and the thrill of his thorough loving. Susie stared at her tear-stained reflection unable to control the pain. It was as if Branch had ripped her heart from her chest and it had shattered into a million pieces. Waves of different emotions smashed into her. She should not have told him about the babies. Maybe if she had waited and formed a more stable relationship with him, he would not have left but how long could she have deceived him? A month maybe two — then what? She hated lying or withholding the truth, but now she would have to live with the consequences of being honest. *I can't win.*

She splashed cold water on her face and dragged leaden feet into the kitchen. Staying up all night waiting for him to return, then being stupid enough to go down to the parking lot to look for his car had been bad enough but getting the nerve to call his cell and discovering the number was out of service had been the last straw. Worry had turned to sobs, and all her insecurities had returned in a rush. He was Branch Durham, handsome, rich and famous. *And me? I am, let's face it, an ugly, fat, pregnant klutz.* Her eyes stung, and the room moved in and out of focus. She needed sleep and nourishment, if not for her for her precious twins. After heating a cup of milk in the microwave, adding chocolate, and sugar, she collapsed onto a chair at the table.

What was wrong with her? She could not get his face out of her mind, his soft drawl, and the words he'd spoken when he made love to her re-ran like a favorite serial on TV. Promises given, hopes dashed. God help her, she could still smell him and her body throbbed from his touch. Anger flared. "What a damn idiot I've been. I am nothing but a booty call to him. Why did he pick me for his games? He could have anyone he wants or is it because he gets a kick out of amusing himself with an inexperienced woman." Her voice echoed in the empty room.

Yet, he had been so gentle, so loving. Had everything he said to her been a lie? She pressed her fingers to lips tingling from his masterful kisses then cupped a breast. Her nipple stiffened under her palm, oversensitive from his suckling. Her body had awakened to him as if remembering his touch and she had loved every second. Pushing both hands through her hair, she sighed, in truth booty call or not, she would fall into his arms again in a second. Although she prided herself for being a strong and independent woman, Branch Durham was a weakness, a crack in her armor she could not repair. She loved him.

"I am such a fool."

Forcing down the warm drink, she placed the cup in the sink then taking up the box of candy headed for the bedroom. She had nowhere to go, no friends to turn to for consolation so she might as well eat candy and mope. Chocolate and ice cream had usually been a remedy for heartache. Later, if sleep refused to come, she could at least lie down and try to regain the positive attitude her mother had told her to adopt. She stared into the dim light. Her mother had been surprisingly supportive as if she had expected her to, as the old folk said, "Get into trouble," the moment she set foot in the USA. Of course, she had the opportunity to return to the UK, but she wanted the twins to be born in America, but if they turned out to be boys, Texas would be the last place she planned to raise them. In fact, the sooner she moved away from men with sexy Texan drawls, the better.

She had time to make up her mind. The apartment belonged to her, and she could sell it for a considerable price. In fact, more than enough for her to purchase a small house in Boston and money to support her while she searched for a new job. Dabbing at a tear with the back of her hand, she tried hard to remain strong and push Branch Durham out of her mind but the idea of losing him hurt so bad. She buried her face in the pillow, and the scent of his aftershave filled her nostrils. The tears flowed. It was time to face facts, nothing would ever erase him from her heart, and when the babies came, she vowed to tell them their father was a hero who saved her life. "Oh, Branch. I love you so much and will forever."

* * * *

Cold seeped through Branch's shirt and for some moments, he fought the heavy fog surrounding his mind. The memory of his kidnappers came back in a rush but the smell of oil replaced the fishy stink of the hood. His hands ached, and he attempted to move fingers swollen by the tight band around his wrists. Head throbbing, he opened his eyes a slit and looked around without moving his head. Oil barrels obscured his view, but from the block and tackle hanging from the ceiling, he assumed the men held him in a garage. He listened intently for any sound of life but heard nothing. High above, sunlight streamed through a broken window, and a breeze rocked dust covered cobwebs. He must have been unconscious for hours, but the foul taste in his mouth and smell wafting from a rag on the floor told him the assholes had used ether to subdue him. Rolling onto his back, he made out the outline of an empty shed. Paint peeled from the walls, dirt, and leaves covered a cracked cement floor.

Wincing he sat up, desperately wanting to touch his face. The tightness on one side seemed to crack as he moved and his head throbbed. He dragged his tongue over dry lips and rested his back against one of the drums. At least they hadn't tied his legs, so he gathered they planned to return before the drug wore off. If the men had left him for the night, likely they would be returning soon, and he would have time to escape. From the soft light and birdsong, it was daybreak. Taking a deep breath, he stood then staggered on wobbly legs to reach the wall and sagged against the old red brick for support. His first priority would be to remove the ties on his wrists. For kidnappers, his did not possess too many brains by leaving him in a garage. He would be sure to find a sharp surface to cut through the plastic and free his hands. Sure enough, after walking not more than six feet, he found a metal workbench and rubbed the cuffs against one edge. When the plastic snapped blood rushed back into his hands. Incredible pain throbbed through his fingers. He stared down at knuckles blue, swollen, and unrecognizable.

Valuable minutes passed as he rubbed his hands together, forcing the circulation back into his fingers. He checked his pockets and found them empty. His thoughts went to Susie and dread cramped his gut. The men had her house keys and could have taken her as well. A motive for his kidnapping slammed into his mind. If Dirk's secretary, Jenny Weeks had been involved, she would have been aware of his visit to Susie and had her address. He had made his search for Susie public, and even though he had not mentioned her by name, he could have placed her in danger. Anger shook him. Fat Guy would know he would pay anything to get her back unharmed. No wonder they had dumped him here, to keep him occupied while they kidnapped his girl. "I'll tear them limb from limb."

The need to get to Susie pushed all other thoughts from his mind. The pain in his head and arms slid into obscurity. He headed for a huge sliding door and using all his strength tried to force it open, but the damn thing would not move an inch. He yelled through the crack. "Hey, let me out of here. You want money I'll get it in one phone call."

Only the whistle of the wind came back through the edge of the door. He jogged toward what looked like the remnants of an office area and bracing for impact shoulder charged the wooden door. Splinters flew in all directions, and the hinges screamed. The door shattered falling to the floor in a giant could of dust. Panting with exertion, he stared at the small kitchenette glimpsing a bathroom down a small corridor and went straight to the sturdy metal door with an "Exit" sign used as a back entrance. From the half circle mark on the floor, the door opened inward. Using all his strength, he pulled on the metal bar, but nothing moved. *I'm trapped.*

He kicked open the entrance to a bathroom. The door bounced against the wall, and he sidestepped the ricochet before the damn thing knocked him on his ass. The place was filthy, unused for many years. A brown rust stain marked the path of a leaking tap in the small porcelain sink, but the dripping water appeared clean. He rubbed his hand over his dry lips then turned on the faucet. Allowing the flow to run and satisfied with its relative safety, he bent ignoring the rush of pain and nausea to wash his face, surprised to see the water run red. Gingerly, he ran the tips of his fingers through his stiff hair and over the crusted gash on one side of his head. A lump the size of an egg lay at the base of his skull. Panic shook his hands at the idea of Susie in the fat man's clutches. He needed to calm down and find a way out of this place. Going crazy would not help either of them. No one would be looking for him either, not for a few days at least. He had made it quite clear to everyone to stay clear. He splashed his face again and licked his lips, no metallic taste or foul odor came from the water. Using both hands as a cup, he drank deeply.

After checking out the bathroom, he used the facilities then climbed onto the toilet seat to peer through a dust-covered window. Maybe he could alert a passerby. His heart dropped at the sight of open fields. He could fit through the window, but the bars would be a problem. He shook them with both hands, but like everything else in the godforsaken place, he could not dislodge them. "Think man." He stomped out of the kitchen stepping over the shattered door and surveyed the littered dusty floor. "There has to be a way out of this place."

The garage was a fortress. He checked every nook and cranny for tools but found nothing. The deep bay under the block and tackle held nothing but empty oil cans. Staring at the chain and the hook dangling from one end, an idea came to him. He jumped up, seized the hook, and dragged the chain to the back door. After attaching the hook to the metal bar used to open the door, he returned to the block and tackle. A machine ran the device and moving the chain through the pulley would lift the incredible weight. Without power, he would have to pull down on the chain and hope the lock holding the door would break. He grasped the chain in both hands, placed one foot in front of the other and pulled. The chain click-clacked through the pulley, and he used all his strength, by swinging on the chain. A loud crack echoed like a gunshot, the pulley whirred, and he fell flat on his back rolling just in time as the chain came crashing down around him. He coughed at the cloud of dust and blinked at the sunlight streaming through the door.

The cut on his head stung, and a trickle of warm blood dripped down his cheek. He pushed to his feet, head swimming and staggered into the early morning sunshine. Shielding his eyes with one hand, he gazed around trying to get his bearings. Dilapidated buildings and a couple of deserted cottages sat nearby. A high fence behind him surrounded an active oil field. He could make out the familiar movement of an oil rig in the distance.

Out front of the garage, a dirt track led to a winding stretch of blacktop not one hundred yards away. The soft soil surrounding the door held two sets of tire tracks and a couple of empty soda bottles. He needed to get far away before the fat man came back and he had to make sure Susie was safe. Scanning the area, he discovered the nearest sign of life was the outline of a barn set at the end of a long line of trees in the distance.

If he ignored the highway and followed the tree line, no one would see him. He looked up at the cloudless sky. It would be a long hot walk. He paused to listen for the sound of a car approaching and sure he had time to spare, collected the discarded soda bottles then dashed back inside, washed and filled them from the tap. With a bottle of water in each hand, he headed out the broken door. Looking all around, he moved off in the direction of civilization and once in the open sprinted for the tree line. "I'm coming, Susie. Hang on, darlin'."

CHAPTER FOURTEEN

Sweat poured a stinging path into Branch's eyes. The distance from the garage to the barn had looked much closer, but after jogging over one mile, he still had a way to go. The temperature was rising with each step and the sun burned through his shirt. Trust him to be stranded miles from anywhere during the hottest fall on record. Add to the fact, he rarely went out without his hat made the journey a misery. Blasts of hot sun cut through the sparse shade from the trees and hit the river blinding him with their brilliance. His soaking clothes stuck to him, and by the time the barn and fences of the ranch came into view, he had consumed most of the water. He caught sight of riders on horseback and broke through the tree line waving his arms. "Hey, over here."

The riders turned and moved toward him at a canter. A young woman with a thin leather-skinned man paused at a gate and observed him with interest. He ran toward them gasping with exhaustion. "Morning, ma'am, sir. My name is Branch Durham, and I need to call nine-one-one."

"Oh, my gosh it is him, Gramps." The young woman turned a spirited palomino and moved closer. "I'm Jinny Morrow, and this is my grandpa, Dale."

"You're covered in blood. What happened to you, son? Did you wreck your car?" Dale leaned down from his mount and unhitched the gate.

"No. I was kidnapped, and my girl is in trouble." He wiped his dry lips with the back of one hand. "I have to get the cops to go check on her."

"Jinny give him your cell phone." Dale held out an arm. "Climb up behind me, son. We'll head for the house. My son is at home, he'll take you anywhere you need to go, might be faster than waiting for the cops to drive out here."

"Yeah, thanks." Branch frowned. "I need to know she is okay."

He climbed onto the horse behind Dale in one easy leap and the massive bay gelding moved off at an infuriatingly slow pace. He took the phone from Jinny's outstretched hand and punched in the number. After explaining to the cops in detail what had happened and asking them to check on Susie. He called Kade and sighed with relief. The kidnappers had not made contact with him, and if they had demanded a ransom from Dirk, his manager would have called. He explained his reasons for believing Miss Weeks was involved. Dirk's secretary was only one of three people aware of him going off the grid for the weekend. No doubt, the men who took him thought they had time to get out of town before contacting his manager or family.

The days of placing, ransom money in paper sacks was over, and now kidnappers demanded payment by electronic transfer. The more sophisticated the operation, the harder it would be to trace funds and find the culprits. He arranged for Kade to collect his spare car keys, contact Dirk then meet him at Susie's apartment. He deleted the contact to his brother, shut the phone, and handed it back to the girl. "Thank you, Jinny."

"Don't you want to call your girl?" Jinny's cheeks pinked.

"I would if I could." Branch wiped a hand down his face and noticed the cut on his head had started bleeding again. "Her number is on the cell phone the kidnappers took from me." He gave her a wry smile. "I've gotten lazy over the years. One time I knew everyone's phone number. Luckily, I know my brother's off by heart." He sighed. "Now we'll all have to get new numbers. I guess my phone will be sold as well."

"Maybe not." Jinny moved her mount closer. "Phones are traceable and could point straight to the men who took you."

Branch nodded, and the small action made him sick to the stomach. With the number of blows to the head, drugs, and dehydration, all he wanted to do was rest. He looked away from the girl trying to avoid conversation and sighed with relief at the sight of a house. They dismounted, and Dale led the way inside. His son, a middle-aged, six-five ball of muscle greeted them in the hallway.

"This is Pete." Dale gave his son a quick rundown of the situation then strode into the kitchen at the end of the hallway.

"I'll grab my keys." Pete pushed on his hat, picked up a bunch of keys from a hook by the front door. "Let's go. I'll have you there in no time flat, and I'll stick around if you need help until the cops arrive."

"Wait up." Dale headed toward Branch and handed him a bottle of water and a couple of energy bars. "Eat something before you fall down."

Branch accepted the welcome gifts and smiled at him. "Thanks, I won't forget your kindness." He followed Pete out the door.

* * * *

Who is hammering in the middle of the night? Susie lifted her head and confused glanced around her room. The noise came from her front door, but no one could get on her floor without her permission. She sat up, swung her legs over the edge of the bed, and reached for her dressing gown. It could not be Branch. He had her house key and would have no need to knock. She sniffed, perhaps the apartment was on fire, although the entire building had fire alarms and apart from the persistent banging, the building was quiet.

A tingle of apprehension crawled up her spine. A woman alone needed to be careful. Moving slowly to the door, she glanced through the peephole. Her stomach clenched at the sight of the badge on a police officer's uniform. She opened the door a crack and peered at the tall figure. "Yes, what is it?"

Two cops and the building supervisor gaped at her as if she had two heads. She gasped at the sight of Branch moving toward her, his handsome face covered with blood, and his clothes filthy. "Oh, my God! What happened to you?"

"I'm fine. It's you we're worried about, darlin'." Branch pushed open the door, gave her a crooked smile then plucked a candy wrapper from her cheek as if seeing her plastered with litter was quite usual. One strong arm circled her waist, and he pulled her against his chest. "Has anyone tried to get inside your apartment?"

Susie's face grew hot with embarrassment at the two police officer's obvious amusement but she walked into the room with Branch, and the cops followed. She shook her head. "No. No one has been here at all. What is going on, Branch, who did this to you?"

"I'll explain everything." He examined her face closely and brushed a kiss across her lips. "I was so worried about you."

One of the cops dismissed the building supervisor and turned to face her, clearing his throat. She ignored him and cast a worried eye over Branch. Under his tan, his face was pale with dark circles under both eyes, and dried blood matted his hair. "You need to see a doctor."

"One is on the way. In fact, quite a few people are heading here. My brother Kade and my manager, Dirk." He glanced down at her. "Can you get dressed and pack a bag? As soon as I've spoken to the officers, I'm taking you to my ranch where it's safe."

She moved away from him and folded her arms over her chest. "I'm not going anywhere until you tell me what the bloody hell happened to you."

"When I left to move the car, I went to the help of a woman, and three armed men mugged then dragged me into a van. I would have taken them on, but one of them held a pistol to my head. The men have your apartment keys. I thought for sure they'd come here and take you as well." Branch placed one heavy arm around her shoulder. "They drugged me and locked me in an abandoned garage, miles away. I escaped early this morning and came straight here. I'm sure glad I left my wallet here, or it would be hell replacing all my credit cards. They have the keys to the Mustang as well. I can't believe it's still outside."

He left his wallet here and car outside. I wish I had known. I would have realized something had happened to him. She frowned. "The car won't be there for long if they come back and steal it."

"It will be fine, there is an officer guarding it at the moment. My brother will be here soon. He has a spare set of keys and will be able to collect my overnight bag from the trunk on the way here." Branch reached for her again and tucked her against his side. "I bet you thought I'd walked out on you again."

Susie leaned into him glad of his solid strength. "The thought did cross my mind."

"You've been crying." He ran a dirty finger down her cheek. "I hurt you again, didn't I?"

"It wasn't your fault." She caught the uncomfortable expressions of the officers and patted him on the arm. "We'll talk later.

He looked so ill, she rubbed his back not sure what to do. "You'd better sit down and wait for the doctor. You don't look so good."

"I'll be fine, but I'm, hot, dirty, and covered in blood." Branch ran the tip of a pink tongue over his cracked lips. "I could sure do with a shower followed by a strong cup of coffee and maybe some toast?"

"Go and take a shower, there's a packet of disposable razors in the top drawer of the vanity, but I don't have any aftershave."

"I'll be fine." Branch rubbed the dark shadow on his chin. "So you like a clean-shaven man, huh?"

"Definitely." She met his amused gaze. "I'll make you some breakfast then I'll pack a bag." She scrutinized the small cuts and bruises on his face and arms. He had a faraway look, and she worried he might be suffering from concussion. "Will you be okay bathing on your own?"

"Sure." He grinned at the cops. "Oh man, I just refused to take a shower with my girl. Maybe the hit on the head did more damage than I thought."

"Behave." She gave him a little push toward the bathroom.

The moment he walked down the hallway she rounded on the officers. "Why didn't you take him straight to the emergency room?"

"He refused medical assistance and insisted we contact his personal physician to meet us here." The blond cop narrowed his gaze. "Mr. Durham was more concerned about your welfare."

"So what are you doing to catch these criminals?"

"One of our detectives is heading over to the ranch to take over the investigation. We take kidnapping very seriously and have reason to believe your life is in danger as well. Going to Mr. Durham's ranch is the best option. You will be safe there."

A shiver crawled up her spine, and she swallowed hard. "If Branch escaped then whoever did this will be long gone. I gather he can't identify them?"

"They wore balaclavas, but he gave us a general description and believes his manager's secretary is involved." The big blond cop looked at her gravely. "From what he said about the isolation of the old garage where the kidnappers held him, we can assume the people responsible have no idea he has escaped. We have a good chance of catching them especially as they have Mr. Durham's cell phone. Our department is in the process of tracking his phone as we speak."

"Has there been any ransom calls?"

"Not as yet." Tall Blond Cop frowned. "We assume they will contact his manager, no doubt using Mr. Durham's phone. We have everything in place waiting for the call."

Susie let out a long sigh. Itching to wash the sticky patch from her cheek, she strolled toward the kitchen. "You might as well wait in the kitchen. I'm sure you'd like a cup of coffee, and I have fresh baked cookies?"

"Thank you, ma'am." Tall Blond Cop grinned at her. "That would be very nice. It's been a long morning."

By the time, Branch emerged from the shower with a towel wrapped around his waist and some nasty bruises showing across his ribs and over his back, Susie had ham, eggs, and a mountain of toast ready for both of them. She sat with him, suddenly hungry and watched him eat with a sense of satisfaction. The cops devoured the plate of cookies, and they all took a second cup of coffee. When Branch pushed back his plate and looked at her, her stomach gave a little twist. "Had enough?"

"That was the finest breakfast I've ever eaten but don't tell Grandma Durham." He covered her hand and met her gaze, his eyes filled with concern. "You look exhausted. I'm so sorry to put you through all this shit."

"It's not your fault." She flicked a gaze over his strong, broad chest and realized he was naked under the towel draped casually around his waist. "Ah . . . do you want me to throw your clothes into the washer? You can't walk around in a towel."

"Kade will be here soon with my bag." He squeezed her hand. "It's going to be a stressful time for you until the cops catch these guys. I want you out of here and safe with me. Pack enough clothes for a few days, anything else you need we'll buy. Take your time, I'm not going anywhere."

Susie touched his face, letting the tips of her fingers caress the bruise on his cheekbone. The idea of a long hot shower was calling her name. "Okay, I'll get ready."

* * * *

Not having that many clothes, Susie packed everything she owned into two suitcases then took a long hot shower. On a ranch, she would need jeans, boots, and a couple of dresses plus something nice to wear if Branch planned to take her on a date. By the time she finished and pulled her suitcases on squeaky wheels toward the sitting room, she could hear the low mumble of male voices. She glanced around at the five men in the room and immediately picked out Branch's brother, Kade. They had the same dark, handsome features and intelligent blue eyes. The uniformed cops had left, and a doctor was spraying an obnoxious smelling spray over the stitches binding the gash in Branch's head.

"You look okay but if you experience any problems with your sight or balance, you call me straight away, and I'll order some scans." The doctor pulled off his gloves and pushed them into a plastic bag filled with bloody dressings. "You are lucky you have a thick skull." He glanced up at her and smiled. "Ah, you must be Susie. John Barnett. Nice to meet you." He patted Branch on the shoulder. "I'll drop by the ranch in ten days to remove the stitches. There is nothing special you need to do. You can take a shower, I've covered the wound with a waterproof dressing."

"Thanks, Doc." Branch held out his hand to her, and she went to him. "Sit with me." He pulled her onto his lap and enclosed her waist with one muscular arm. "This is my brother, Kade, my manager, Dirk, and Detective Wells. The bad news is they haven't traced my phone, so these criminals are smarter than we think. We'll head home and leave the police to do their job."

"They'll have to turn on the cell phone sooner or later to gain access to the numbers unless they call Dirk on the landline, but either way, we have the numbers covered. One of our men will take the call and attempt to keep them on the line for as long as we need to set up a trace." Detective Wells got to his feet. "If you're ready to leave, the officers outside will escort you to your vehicle."

Susie glanced at Branch, loving the feel of his hard body pressing against her. "Are we taking my car?"

"Nope." Branch grinned at her worried expression. "Kade brought my spare set of keys." He chuckled. "Don't worry, if you need your car, I'll have one of my men collect it for you, but before you come back here, I'm having the locks changed. I've organized a locksmith, and the building supervisor will handle everything." He lifted her off his lap. "Come on, darlin', I'm taking you home."

CHAPTER FIFTEEN

The ride in the Mustang was fast and furious, leaving the other men way behind. Susie loved muscle cars, and the roar of the engine thrilled her. She had confidence in Branch's driving, if he could maneuver a motorcycle through the devastation of a hurricane, he could handle a road just fine. Her breath caught as they left the highway, traveled some way down a side road then turned a corner. In front of them, a massive white gate swung open to reveal a modern picturesque ranch house at the end of a long driveway. On each side, glossy horses roamed white fenced paddocks and rolling open land spread out as far as the eye could see. When Branch drove the car into a huge garage, she noticed his precious Indian motorcycle was one of a huge collection of vehicles. Rows of polished chrome and paintwork filled an area the size of an aircraft hangar. The massive doors closed behind them, and she swallowed hard as the magnitude of Branch's wealth hit her. *I'm not ever going to fit in here.*

"You have that look again." Branch unclipped his seat belt, unfastened hers and pulled her into his arms. "What is troubling you, darlin'?"

How could she explain? She gazed at his battered face and sighed. The truth was the best option. "I'm not sure I'll fit in here. I'm a simple girl, I work for a living, and all this is a bit overwhelming."

"I've had money all my life. My grandpa hit oil here many years ago, but I'm still the same person you met on a beach in Florida." He cupped her face in his warm hands. "I'm still your Branch, the man you went through hell and back with and the father of our babies. Money makes life easy in some ways harder in others, but it doesn't change *who* I am inside." He brushed soft kisses over her mouth. "Forget all the trappings, and kiss me, darlin', I want you so bad."

"Oh, Branch. I'm so worried about making a fool of myself in front of your family. I can be so clumsy." She wanted to say more, but he covered her mouth with a feral moan and devoured her.

She melted against him, opening her mouth and returning his passion. He tasted of coffee and smelled of her green apple body wash, but his masculine scent broke through as if calling to her basic instincts. She craved him. Their tongues tangled in a familiar dance and when his hand slid under her shirt to tweak her sensitive nipples, she arched toward him. His kiss deepened, and she clung to him panting with delight. When he broke the kiss and bared her breasts then took one nipple into his hot, wet mouth she cried out in ecstasy. His sharp teeth scraped over the hard tip driving her insane, but when he slid one hand up her thigh and pulled at her panties, she came to her senses. "Someone will see us."

"No they won't. It's safe here." He leaned across her and opened the door. "Do you want me, darlin'?"

She wet her lips, and the action caught his full attention. "Yes."

"I can't wait until everyone leaves us alone, can you?" He pushed one finger inside her panties and circled her clit. "You are so wet."

Her hips had a mind of their own and pushed up to meet his exploring fingers. "There's not enough room to do anything here."

"I know. Get out of the car."

She complied, and he followed her and pulled her into his strong arms. He kissed her again, long, deep, and slow then turned her toward the hood of the car. She glanced at him over one shoulder, excitement thrumming through her at what he was contemplating. "Here and from behind?"

"Uh-huh. I'm planning to have your sweet pussy everywhere on my ranch. Being naughty is fun. Trust me you'll love how deep I can get inside you." He slid her skirt up to her waist and her silk panties dissolved in his hands. "Bend over and open those pretty thighs for me." One hand slid around her to caress her slick folds. "So wet."

She heard his belt unhitch and his zipper slide down then the heat of him pressed against her. He surrounded her, blocking out any reservations. She trusted him and wiggled her bottom against his bare hard flesh. When he entered her in one mind-blowing slide, she rested her hands on the warm metal of the car and sighed with contentment. He took her in long hard thrusts, each time plunging deeper inside her. She pushed back to meet him stroke for stroke rocking her hips to take every tantalizing inch of him. He filled her, so hot and thick igniting undiscovered nerve endings with erotic euphoria.

"So beautiful. I love watching your tits bounce in the shine on my car. Hmm, now I want to have you in front of a mirror. Come for me, darlin'." Branch swirled his hips. "Squeeze me tight."

She wanted the amazing sensations to last forever, but his deep sexy voice sent flames of desire curling in her belly. In a few sensational moments, her legs shook, and wave after wave of delicious orgasm rushed over her. He moaned his appreciation and drove into her then in a rush of heat reached his own conclusion. The next second, he slipped from her turned her around and lifted her onto the hood of the car then stepped between her knees and pushed inside her again. Gasping she leaned back on her palms. Her shirt hung open, and he fell on her full breasts taking one then the other tingling nipple deep in his mouth. He rocked his hips, and his still-hard length sent waves of delight inside her. Growling deep in his throat, he suckled her breasts and reignited her passion. The way he used his soft lips and dragged his teeth across her sensitive flesh had her rising to climax again. The moment, he ground his hips hard against her clit, another orgasm rushed through her.

"Oh yeah, that's my girl." He pulled her toward him and claimed her mouth.

Breathless, she wallowed in his afterglow kisses. A long time later, he lifted her from the hood and carried her into a small bathroom. He cleaned her gently, washed her face, and rearranged her clothes with such tenderness tears stung the backs of her eyes.

Horns sounded from close by, and he rolled up his eyes. She giggled. "The others have arrived."

"They have probably been here for a while." He grinned and smoothed her hair. "I *could* get you a pair of panties from your bag but I'd rather you didn't wear any. It will be our secret, okay?"

Her face grew hot, and the idea made her feel naughty, but after having amazing sex on the hood of a Mustang and enjoying every second, she would go with the flow. "Okay."

Branch collected the bags from the trunk of the car then using the keypad punched in the code to enter the house. He ignored the chatter coming from the den and took Susie straight to his bedroom. "Do you wanna share with me, darlin'? I have six bedrooms if you'd rather be alone."

"Let me think." Susie tapped her bottom lip and stared at the ceiling. "Stay with the man with an insatiable sex drive or sleep alone? Decisions, decisions." She giggled and poked one finger at his chest. "I'll sleep with you and keep you safe just in case the bad man tries to kidnap you again."

"Hmm, maybe you should tie me to the bed, huh?" He moved closer and licked her ear. "I'll teach you how to ride, Branch style."

"Like I said, insatiable." Susie slid both hands under his shirt sending goose bumps over his flesh. "Later, right now I'm exhausted, and we need to find out if there's been any ransom demands." She glanced at the room. "Nice place and that bed is huge. I'll lose you in there."

"I promise you won't." He smiled down at her. "In case it slipped your memory, I like to spoon."

Allowing her time to look around, he lifted her bags onto the bed then opened the door to his walk-in closet. "I'll tell my housekeeper to unpack your things."

"Oh, no you won't." Susie gave him a horrified look. "If I'm staying in here with you then this room is out of bounds. I am quite capable of taking care of us."

He shook his head. "Nope. I'm not having you changing linen or cleaning floors. We'll discuss what you want to do if you must help around the house but you're pregnant, and I'm taking care of you, so be a good girl." Moving close, he touched her cheek. "You might hate staying with me and want to hightail it to some safe house arranged by the cops. In the meantime, let me do this . . . please?"

"Okay, but she won't walk in on us, will she?" Susie's eyes flashed and her cheeks pinked. "I like my privacy."

He pulled her close and slid one hand under her skirt to cup her smooth bottom. "My staff are like ghosts. They have their own living quarters and times to do things. I plan to have sex with you in every room, but I'll work around their schedule." Loving the way, her skin pebbled against his palm, he grinned down at her. "I guess we'd better go and see what's happening in the den. I gather the cops are setting up in there to wait for the ransom call."

"You are so calm about all this, Branch." Susie took the hand he offered and followed him from the room. "I'm worried. They had guns, and I didn't see any guards at your gate. What if they discover you've escaped and come here?"

"I don't think they'd risk showing up here." He squeezed her hand. "They would have to walk a hell of a long way to get here and would likely trip a few sensors along the way. I have a security firm monitoring the ranch. There are cameras everywhere, and from the highway, the only way to the house is through the main gate. We're safe here, promise."

Inside the den, the mood was somber. Dirk and a number of strangers sat around his desk with laptops and gadgets. Surprised to see two of his brothers waiting for him, he led Susie toward Hunter. "Susie, this is my brother, Hunter. There is one more Durham boy, Lance but he is at school."

"Nice to meet you." Hunter swept his gaze over her then met Branch's gaze with a raised brow. "Nothing is happening yet, no word from the assholes who kidnapped you but I need a word with you — in private."

Susie took in the tall, handsome man dressed in a very expensive business suit. Hunter looked nothing like a cowboy. Unnerved by the way he dismissed her without as much as offering a handshake she stepped closer to Branch. The movement caught Hunter's complete attention, and the glare he gave Branch spoke volumes. *He hates me already.*

"Why don't you take a seat, missy?" Hunter indicated with his chin to a long leather sofa. "I have business to discuss with Branch, and I'm afraid it won't wait."

"Her name is Susie." Branch stepped between them. "What's your problem?"

The next moment Kade was at her side. He gave her an apologetic smile and offered his arm like a Lord in a historical movie. "You look exhausted. There is a fresh pot of coffee in the kitchen, come with me, and I'll pour you a cup."

She slipped her hand on his thick muscular arm and smiled. "Thank you, I didn't get much sleep last night."

"Well then rather than dragging you in here, maybe Branch should have showed you to a room to rest." Kade chuckled. "You see, he lives very strange hours and forgets normal people need sleep."

Coming to his defense at once, she lifted her chin. "He did show me to a room, but I wanted to find out what was happening."

Seated at a huge marble-topped center island in a kitchen straight from a glossy magazine, Susie sipped coffee. She could hear muffled voices, which became louder as Branch and Hunter moved closer. Her face grew hot with embarrassment as it became obvious she was the topic of conversation.

"It's not bad enough you bring your hussy here, but by the look of the pair of you, it's obvious you had sex in the garage. If you tell me you needed stress relief after last night's fiasco, I'll knock you down." Hunter's voice, deep and treacherous cut into her like a thousand knives. "Then you parade her in front of the cops. Have you lost your mind? You both stink of sex, and they are not stupid. If they don't arrest you for having sex with an underage girl, one of them will earn some extra bucks by leaking it, and the story will be all over the media by morning."

"You are so going to regret making insinuations about my girl." Branch's voice was low and menacing. "I can find investments elsewhere you know."

"I'm the only one who will save you from yourself, Branch, and you damn well know it." Hunter cleared his throat. "Let me deal with her."

"*Deal* with her? Good Lord!" Branch's footsteps echoed outside the kitchen door. "I'm a grown man, and you're not my pa, so back off, Hunter."

When the men burst into the kitchen, Susie dropped her head in shame. She sensed Branch behind her before his warm hand rested on her shoulder. Without a second thought, she covered his hand offering her unspoken support and gazed up at his exasperated expression.

"Susie, I know it's very impolite of me, but would you mind informing my brother how old you are, darlin'?"

Anger flared at the idea. Did Hunter truly believe his brother had bedded an underage girl? He must believe his brother was lower than an alley cat, but she knew different. Especially the way Branch had kept his distance at first and made a not so subtle point of discovering her age at the get-go. Yes, she had to admit she had to confirm her age many times but being youthful was an advantage most women would crave.

Ignorance was no excuse for Hunter's rudeness, and pregnancy hormones obviously turned women into warriors because as sure as hell, she refused to take his shit a moment longer. She straightened and eyed him with all the contempt she could muster. "Maybe you should close the door and sit down." She flicked a glance at Branch. "I thought you said your family would welcome me? So far, Hunter has looked at me as if I'm some sleazy streetwalker you hired for a porno flick." She pushed to her feet and held up a hand to silence the two angry men. "I refuse to validate the reason I'm staying with Branch, but I *can* fix this problem. I'm going to ask the cops to put me in a safe house until they have caught the kidnappers. I am not in the habit of breaking up families, and I'm not starting now." With trembling knees, she headed for the door, but Branch grasped her arm and turned her to face him.

"Don't get upset. Hunter refuses to believe me, but then I am the black sheep of the family. He is the one who keeps me on the straight and narrow." Branch frowned down at her. "Oh my God, you are sheet-white."

The room moved in and out of focus, and she gripped the back of the chair. Oh, shit if she fainted she would make a bigger fool of herself. The next moment, Branch had her in his strong arms. He sat down with her, and she rested her aching head against his chest.

"See what you've done." Branch glared at Hunter. "Not only is she twenty-one, but she is also pregnant, and yeah the babies are mine."

"Babies?" Hunter dragged a hand through his dark hair, and his expression showed his disbelief.

"What babies?" Kade shot to his feet and stared at her with raised brows. "Is this true, Susie?"

Susie lifted her head away from the comforting thump of Branch's heartbeat and nodded. "Yes, I'm twenty-one, and I'm having twins."

"You haven't seen her in almost five months." Hunter narrowed his eyes to slits and his brow furrowed. "No way, man. This is a setup, and you're allowing your cock to rule your head." He shot a dark look at her. "How much do you want to walk out of his life?"

"Absolutely nothing." Susie swallowed the lump in her throat. "I'll sign any paperwork you want, but then I'm leaving."

A tremble went through Branch and he pounded his fist so hard on the table the coffee mugs overturned and rolled crashing to the floor.

"Enough. How dare you come into my home and speak to her like that?" Branch lifted her gently to her feet and stood. "We knew you'd all react like this, so before you flap your lips and do any more damage, I suggest you wait for the paternity test, which we are doing for no other reason but to satisfy the family." He glared at his brothers. "I *know* the babies are mine."

A knock on the door ended any further discussion. One of the detectives stepped into the kitchen and flicking a concerned gaze over them spoke softly.

"The ransom call just come in. Dirk is handling it very well. He is playing for time, but we already have a fix on your phone — thank God for technology. They are in DC. I mean how stupid can you get? The cybercrime unit there is incredible."

"How much am I worth?" Branch lifted his chin.

"Three million, and Dirk told them he couldn't arrange the transfer until the bank opens on Monday. They said once they confirmed the deposit they would call with your location. The FBI are closing in on the phone's coordinates." The detective smiled. "Unless they are smarter than we think, it should all be over soon."

"Thanks." Branch shook his hand. "I hope we can keep this out of the media."

"I'll do my best." The detective nodded slowly. "We'll be out of your hair as soon as we get confirmation of an arrest."

"Yeah, and make sure you include Jenny Weeks, she is involved. She was the only other person apart from Dirk and Kade who knew I visited Susie. I'm pretty sure she was the woman they used to trap me." He sighed. "If I hadn't wanted something out of my car, they wouldn't have gotten the chance to kidnap me. I did what any man would do in the same situation. I saw a woman fall over and went to help her."

"Dumb luck, huh?" The detective grimaced.

"It seems that way." Branch rubbed his chin. "I'm a sucker for ladies in distress." He grinned. "That's how I met Susie."

The detective gave her a long considering stare then raised both brows. "Ah, you're the girl he saved from the hurricane? Have you seen the spread in that woman's magazine? That was an amazing story. Although, you look a lot different from that scared kid nestled under Branch's arm at the shelter. No wonder Hunter here thought you were underage."

Susie opened her mouth to say something then shut it at Kade's peals of laughter.

"Welcome to the crazy world of Branch Durham." Kade flashed her a white grin. "The story was pure fiction, but speculation Susie is the same girl he took to the shelter was ignited by Branch's plea to find his mermaid."

"Looks like he found you." The detective chuckled. "Trust Branch to get himself kidnapped the same day. I'm surprised you didn't hightail it back to the UK. Trouble follows him, don't you know?"

It would seem the detective had the inside story on her life. She glanced at Branch, and when his passionate, hungry gaze licked over her, her womb gave a little twist of recognition. It happened every time he looked at her, and the way he licked his lips was so sexy, no every damn movement he made sent her hormones raging. She loved him, and the way he protected her from his brothers made her believe he had feelings for her too. *I hope so.* When he winked at her, she wanted to jump into his arms for a thorough loving. She dragged her eyes away from him and met the detective's stare.

"So I gathered, and it hasn't stopped with the kidnapping, has it Branch?"

"Darlin', you are the kind of trouble I enjoy handling." Branch moved behind her and pulled her against him. His voice dropped to a whisper, and warm breath brushed her neck. "You look exhausted. Why don't you rest before lunch? I'm not going anywhere."

Stressed out to the max and with the tension between the brothers so thick she could cut it with a knife, she leaned into him. Escaping from Hunter's glare and the chance of a short nap would be bliss. "Thanks. I will, but you should rest too, you have a head injury."

"I'll be fine." Branch gave her a little squeeze. "I want to see this ransom demand through first and have a long talk to my brothers." He brushed a kiss over her cheek. "I'll sort everything out, you don't have to worry."

Susie bit back a yawn and dragged leaden legs toward the hallway. Tired did not come close to the complete exhaustion weighing down her shoulders. She welcomed the cool quiet of Branch's room, pushed her bags from the bed, and flopped down. When Branch's scent enveloped her, an easy calm descended, and she closed her eyes. *I'm safe.*

CHAPTER SIXTEEN

Branch waited for the detective to leave the room and pushed the kitchen door shut before rounding on his brothers. Keeping his voice low, he moved in close. "You have Susie all wrong. She knew I've been trying to find her and rather than make me believe she was after my money, decided not to tell me about the babies." He rubbed one hand down his face. The idea his girl had not trusted him enough to tell him hurt like hell. "She told me to walk away." He looked at one bemused expression to the other. "I had to convince her to give me a chance, and when I bring her here, you two act like idiots. Fuck! Don't you think she's been through enough?"

"I didn't say a word to her. In fact, I've been a perfect gentleman." Kade lifted his chin. "Hunter is just looking out for you. Heck, Branch, we both thought she was underage. I can't believe she is twenty-one."

"What do you mean by 'she's been through enough'? What's going on we don't know about?" Hunter rubbed his chin. "Give me details, Branch."

As if all his energy had seeped out, Branch dropped into a chair and reached for the coffee pot. "The truth is, I wanted her from the get-go. The moment I saved her from drowning, I knew she was someone very special, innocent, and best of all she figured I was a beach bum." He poured coffee into his empty cup and let out a long sigh. "Being with someone normal, someone beautiful and innocent was amazing. She sees me as Branch a simple cowboy, not some superstar millionaire with shares in Durham Oil."

"Hang on a minute. *Innocent?*" Hunter sat opposite and glared at him. "Oh, Lord, you took her virginity, didn't you? So now you feel obligated to care for her. *You* need professional help."

"You didn't force yourself on her, did you?" Kade sat on the edge of the table and glared at him. "What other reason could you possibly have for not using protection?"

Branch held up both hands. "Hell, no."

"'Hell, no' you didn't take her virginity or 'hell, no' you didn't forget to use protection?" Hunter eyed him over the rim of his cup. "Either way you are in deep shit, brother."

Inhaling the rich aroma of coffee, Branch tried to gather his wits, which remained scrambled from the mugging. "We went through a life and death situation during the hurricane. I guess I shouldn't have made love to her, but she asked me and hell, it could have been our last minutes on earth." He sipped the hot brew. "I used protection, but we became attached very fast, and things between us became pretty intense. Things happen — okay? It was not as if I could find a pharmacy. The entire place was flattened."

"You didn't answer my question." Hunter ran the tip of one finger around the top of his mug.

"That's because it's none of your damn business." Branch pushed down the need to punch his brother hard on the nose. "Or what has happened since she arrived here. I mean finding out about the babies makes no difference. I *love* her. It came on me the day after we met in a rush so intense I couldn't make sense of it, but we've been apart for four months, and I still burn for her. I need her in my life and to be honest, if the babies turn out not to be mine, I don't care. I will love them because they are part of *her*." He cleared the lump in his throat. "But they *are* mine. I feel like a heel to have done the calculations in my head, but I guess that's natural."

"Okay." Hunter shrugged. "Then we won't speak of this again, but you'll have to tell Grandma before she sees it on the news."

"Not about the twins, not until the tests come back. I know she'll want proof. The rest I can handle, for now, so I expect you both to keep your mouths shut." Bone weary, Branch slumped in his chair. "When all this is over, and I have my home back to myself, I'll need to spend time with Susie."

"Grandma will expect you to marry her. She has wanted one of us to get married and have kids before she dies." Kade drummed his fingers on the table. "Has the idea even entered your mind?"

"Every waking moment." Branch rubbed the back of his neck. Hell, he had yet to tell Susie he loved her. "She might not want me, have you thought about that?" He cupped the mug of coffee, and a wave of despair washed over him. "She is independent, a little clumsy, and tells me like it is. I need someone like her in my life, but she'll run away again if the family try and pressure her."

"Then what are you going to do?" Hunter frowned. "You have a responsibility to those babies."

"Yeah, but rushing Susie into accepting a proposal of marriage won't work. She isn't the kind of woman to agree to marry me for the twins' sake. I'll take things one day at a time and hope she falls in love with me." He drew a deep breath. "Whatever happens, I plan to be a father to my kids."

* * * *

Susie stretched, and the warm, heavy arm around her waist tightened. "Are you awake?"

"Ah-huh." Branch cupped her breast and tweaked the sensitive nipple.

"Did the cops arrest the guys who mugged you?"

"They arrested three men and Jenny Weeks. They will have to arrange to bring them back to Dallas to face charges. They have my statement, and one of the guys is singing like a bird for a deal."

"That's good." She smiled into the darkness, and her stomach growled. "I'm starving."

"Me too." Branch splayed his fingers over her belly. "You didn't tell me the twins were moving."

Rolling onto her back, she looked at him. "No, they're not. Well, I don't think they are yet. It's probably wind."

"Nope, it's them. I just know it is and they know me already." He chuckled. "There — did you feel that? Like a butterfly's wings?"

She covered his large hand and lay very still. The fluttering came again, and she smiled. "I think you're right, but that's the first time I've noticed anything." She glanced at the window. "It's dark already. What time is it?"

"We slept through the afternoon." He raised up on one elbow. "I came in here to check on you after the cops left. Your skirt was hitched up showing the curve of your sexy ass, and I couldn't leave." He grinned at her and moved his hand to cup her bottom. "It took all my willpower not to wake you. You are so beautiful, and I want to make love to you all the time."

Her stomach growled, and she giggled. "You would tempt a Saint, but I need a shower and something to eat. I haven't forgotten Hunter's remark about smelling like sex."

"I'm sorry. Hunter's behavior was unforgivable, but he is the smart one in the family and tries to protect me. I didn't have time to explain about you, and as he expects me to be the black sheep, he jumped to the wrong conclusion."

"Black sheep, huh?" She chewed on her bottom lip and caught the flash of concern in his eyes. "Do you make a habit of bringing home underage girls sans panties?"

"No, I swear." He crossed his heart. "When we first met, I thought you might be seventeen, but with all the sand it was difficult to tell. I liked you fine but would have asked the old couple to look after you rather than risk temptation and, darlin', you are *sooo* damn tempting."

A wave of awareness flamed up her inner thighs. "Being over twenty-one obviously has its benefits." She ran the tip of her finger over his full, soft lips and smiled. "Will your brothers be a problem? I really like Kade. He is a lot like you. Hunter is aggressive and scares the hell out of me."

"Don't worry your pretty head about my brothers." He rolled off the bed and stretched showing a delicious line of tanned skin under his tee shirt. "They won't come by unless we invite them." He held out his hand. "Forget them, let's take a shower. There is a casserole in the fridge and a loaf of fresh bread when we're done."

Susie slid from the bed and followed him into the bathroom. "That sounds wonderful. You are going to spoil me."

"Darlin', I haven't started yet."

Branch shed his clothes and turned to help Susie undress. He pulled her to him enjoying the graze of taut nipples against his chest and kissed her. When she cupped the back of his neck and nibbled along his chin, his resolve to prove he wanted more from her than sex vanished. He devoured her mouth and used his tongue to caress and tease. By the time he lifted his head, Susie's eyes had become unfocused with passion. He had no doubt she found him attractive, and gave himself a mental shake then turned on the water. "I'll wash your back." He followed her into the cubicle and pumped shower gel into the palm of one hand.

"That would be nice." Susie soaped up her hair then glanced at him over one shoulder. "I can't wait to see your ranch. I love horses, and yours look beautiful."

He made swirls of soap suds over her back then moved his hands around to lather her breasts. "I'll give you the grand tour in the morning." He washed her belly and groaned. "What do you want to do tonight?" He pushed down the desire to spread her legs and slip deep inside her.

"I'd like to see the rest of the house." When she turned in his arms and reached for the soap, he stilled her hand. She frowned up at him. "What's wrong?"

Wishing his rampant desire for her was not so damn obvious he rested his forehead on her brow and sighed. "You make me crazy. Before we met, I didn't have the urge to make love every waking moment. Now, I only have to look at you and I get hard."

"Is that a bad thing?"

He pulled her against him. "Lord, no, but I don't want you to think I only want you for sex." When she made a groan of protest, he gazed into her deep blue eyes and did not miss the look of rejection. "I took your virginity and ignited a craving. I should know better, but when I'm with you, I'm like a starving man and you're the finest banquet." He caressed her back and moved her under the warm water. "I want you to get to know me. You might not like the man I am or the life I am forced to lead."

"I've seen the real Branch Durham." Susie tipped back her head and rinsed the shampoo from her long blonde hair. "Money, fame, the paparazzi or anything else in your life won't change my opinion of you." She moved out from under the flow, folded her arms over her fine breasts and observed him. "Is that the real reason you wanted me to come here?"

"Nope." He used the shower gel then rinsed off the suds. "I missed you, have missed you since the hurricane."

Following her from the shower, he waited for her to turn to face him. "I've wanted a relationship with you since the first day we met, but it would be impossible out in the real world." He snatched a towel off the shelf and wrapped it around his waist. "Some people go out of their way to cause trouble, and trust me, you'd be a target. I thought the kidnapping was a start of the media discovering I'd found you."

"I see." Susie wrapped a towel around her hair. "So, you want us to be *just friends*, no sex?"

"Hell no." He cupped her chin loving the indignation in her eyes. "I want to make love to you in every room in this house. I'm saying, stay with me here on the ranch so you can see if you like me outside the bedroom."

"One minute." Susie's mouth curled into a wicked smile. She pulled the towel from his waist then gave him a slow appraisal from toes to head. "Well, I still like you in here, and I absolutely loved you in the garage." She handed him the towel. "As to staying here. I have a new job, and I am supposed to start on Monday, so you'll have to take me home tomorrow."

Branch snorted and gripped her gently by the upper arms. "Is the job the only reason you want to leave me?"

"Of course, I need to support my babies."

"You don't need a job. I'll support you, and if you go home, I'll miss you." He rubbed her arms. "Plus, the media will hound you day and night. Here you are safe, and I come as an added bonus. *Please,* Susie. Stay with me, and if I turn out to be intolerable, I will take you home, but I will support you either way. I need to be in the twins' lives. Will you at least agree to allow me to be involved?"

"Of course I will, Branch. They are your babies too, and I wouldn't stop you seeing them, but I can't sit around here all day painting my toenails." Susie chewed on her bottom lip. "What will I do when you're on tour?"

He pushed both hands through his hair then kissed the tip of her nose. "I need a new PA. I'm sure you wouldn't want me spending time with another woman, and PA's usually live here." He licked the corners of her mouth and sighed when her tongue flicked out to meet his. "On tour, you and the twins will be with me — or I won't tour."

"Okay, I'll stay." Susie brushed a warm kiss over his lips. "Now can we eat?"

CHAPTER SEVENTEEN

The following day, Susie led the way into the gynecologist's rooms, and Dr. Jessica Wright took the samples for the paternity test. As she lay back on the examination couch watching the ultrasound screen, Branch squeezed her hand so tight her bones rubbed together. To her delight, he asked questions about the twins, how he could care for her, and the delivery classes. He was a man of his word and wanted complete involvement with the babies.

"You seem so excited about the babies, Mr. Durham, so I have to ask why the need for a paternity test?" The doctor handed Susie a wad of tissues to wipe away the ultrasound gel then raised a brow at Branch.

"I know the twins are mine." Branch smiled at Susie with such sweetness her heart skipped a beat. "The test is to eliminate any gossip or innuendo as we were apart for four months. People can be cruel."

"Then it's an excellent idea. As you are paying for the express pathology, they should be back in four to five days. I will call Susie the moment they arrive and have a copy of the results sent out to you by courier as requested." Dr. Wright turned her attention back to Susie. "Do you want to know the twins' sex? They are identical, and it will come back with the results, but some couples prefer to wait."

Susie looked at Branch who was nodding like one of those dogs people place on dashboards. She giggled. "Yes, we would love to know the sex."

"They're boys." Branch flicked a glance at the doctor and shrugged. "There hasn't been a girl born in our family in five generations."

"But I'm not a Durham." Susie frowned at him. "Would it be a problem if they are girls?"

"Honey, I'd love them just the same and hoped they look like you." He bent to brush a kiss over her lips. "But they *are* boys just look at those long legs — my legs."

"I'll have a copy of the image ready for you by the time you leave." Dr. Wright smiled at her. "You are doing fine but make sure you put your feet up after lunch every day. Make an appointment to see me in one month, from then I'll need to see you once a week." She turned and strolled from the examination room.

"Are you ready to visit my grandma? She will know all about you by now, and if I don't drop by the house and pay her a visit, there will be hell to pay. She rules the roost at the Durham Ranch."

Susie giggled. "No wonder your brothers haven't married."

* * * *

Later that morning, Susie gathered her courage and walked into the kitchen of the Durham Ranch. A gray-haired woman with beautiful features sat at the kitchen table shucking peas and resembled someone out of yesteryear. With Branch's hand firmly on her waist, Susie stepped through the door and waited for the woman to lift a remarkable dark blue gaze to her.

"Grandma, I'd like you to meet Miss Susan Blake formally of Boston." Branch moved toward the table and pulled out a chair for her. "Sit yourself down, darlin', I'm sure my Grandma has a million questions." He strolled to the coffee maker, took down cups, and turned his back.

Oh, great! "It's very nice to meet you. Branch has told me so much about you."

"He's told me diddly squat about *you*." Grandma Durham pushed the bowl of peas to one side and observed her keenly.

"You're the first girl he's dragged over my front door to meet me. How old are you?"

Taken aback by her bluntness, Susie swallowed hard. "Twenty-one."

"Uh-huh. That sure doesn't sound like a Boston accent to me. Who are your people?"

"My mother is English but her maiden name was Beal, her father was born in Boston." She tried to push down the awful lump constricting her throat. "They lived in Boston but divorced, and my mother returned to the UK."

"What brought you to Dallas?"

After Susie explained about her job managing her father's condominium block and meeting Branch, she had calmed down a little. When Branch served the coffee, sat down, and held her hand under the table her courage returned, but to her dismay, he kept out of the conversation. She flicked him a "help me" gaze, and he answered her plea with a grin.

"My ma told me not to marry a sailor because they have a woman in every port." Grandma Durham leaned forward in her chair and peered at her. "Branch thinks I don't know, but he has had more girlfriends in more towns than I've had hot dinners."

"That's true enough, and Susie is fully aware of my past." Branch leaned back in his chair making the wood creak. "But how many have I introduced to you? My tomcatting days are over, Susie is special, and I want to keep her."

Susie gaped at him. *Oh, my God, he wants to keep me.*

"She's not a puppy, Branch. You can't play with her for a while then give her to someone else when you get bored." Grandma Durham raised both brows and shook her head. "Does her father know she is staying at your ranch with you unchaperoned?"

"Nope." Branch turned the coffee mug around in his long fingers. "After what happened to me, it's safer for her at my ranch, and people don't have chaperones anymore. She's not a beauty pageant contestant." He met his grandmother's gaze with a belligerent stare. "I have six bedrooms, Grandma, and you know darn well, I don't usually make a habit of allowing women to stay at my ranch. This is different. Susie is a special lady."

Oh, wow. Susie glanced at him and smiled linking her fingers through his. Her face grew hot under Grandma Durham's inquisitive stare. "Branch is special to me too, and we need some time alone to see if we fit together. As you know, Branch saved my life, and I think he believes I am suffering from hero worship. In his line of work, I guess he has to deal with women who don't look beneath the image to see the man."

"Susie doesn't follow Country and Western music and didn't recognize me. She believed I was a beach bum, and during the hurricane we became very close." Branch sighed. "If the family could back off for a couple of weeks, we might discover if we actually *like* each other."

"I guess that's the modern way of doing things." Grandma Durham sipped her coffee and eyed them over the rim of the bone china floral cup. "It's like shutting the gate after the horse has bolted but whatever you decide is fine by me."

"Good." Branch pushed to his feet. "I've promised to give Susie a tour of the ranch. I'll see you for Sunday dinner as usual."

"See that you do." Grandma Durham smiled at Susie. "You are welcome at my table anytime, missy."

Susie stood and met the old woman's gaze. *She knows I'm pregnant. I'm sure.* "Thank you. I'll look forward to seeing everyone again."

Relieved to have the meeting over they headed back to the car. Once they were on their way, she turned to Branch. "That was a little intense. Is she usually like that?"

"Yeah." Branch started the car, and they headed down the long driveway. "After our parents died, she took over raising four wild boys. It hasn't been easy for her because we are all different."

"Tell me about your brothers."

"Hunter has a law degree and a business degree and is the CEO of Durham Oil. The rest of us boys are shareholders in both the company and Durham Ranch. Kade is a pilot and a cattleman. He likes to manage that side of things and enjoys riding the rodeo circuit. He is the true cowboy of the family. I just play at being a cowboy these days." He turned the car into the long driveway leading to his home. "Lance is at college, he is business all the way like Hunter, and his future is with Durham Oil."

As they reached the front of the house, she smiled at him. "You all look alike. Is that from your father?"

"Yeah, we all look like Dad, but my mom had the same coloring, dark hair and blue eyes." He drove into the garage. "What do you want to see first?"

She grinned at him. "The horses."

* * * *

After an hour of exploring the ranch and introducing Susie to the staff, Branch walked her back to the house. He wanted her to take the doctor's advice and rest after lunch. "I told Milly not to come by the house today. I want to look after you, and I do cook a mean grilled cheese sandwich we can have for lunch. There are steaks in the fridge for dinner, if you can throw together a salad later, I'll fire up the barbecue."

"That sounds wonderful." Susie followed him to the mudroom and joined him at the sink. "When do I get to meet the elusive housekeeper? Is she a busty redhead you're hiding from me?"

He grinned at her liking the streak of jealousy. "Come to think of it she is busty but I think her husband would be a little annoyed if I looked at her the wrong way, plus she is old enough to be my mother."

"That's good." Susie led the way into the kitchen. "You know, you've told me everything about your home and family but nothing about your career." She filled the coffee maker. "I've haven't heard you hum or whistle, and you write your own songs, don't you? Do the lyrics come into your head, and you have to write them down before they slip away?"

He pulled sandwich fixings out the refrigerator and placed them on the bench. "Yeah, it happens like that, different things trigger a song. I have a music room downstairs beside the cinema where I can work undisturbed." He took out a pan and placed it on the stove.

"You have a cinema?" Susie gaped at him then as if trying to cover her amazement buttered slices of bread. "Of course you do. All this place needs is a shopping mall, and it would be self-sufficient."

Damn! He touched her cheek, and her amazing blue gaze slid over his face. "You know I can't go to the movies like a regular guy. I can take you to quite a few restaurants but being me isn't easy and being my girl won't be easy either. I have fans who are jealous of the women I date, and I want to protect you from them. Once they know about you, the hate mail will start."

"I had no idea they were so possessive." Susie shook her head. "That's awful like having a group of stalkers."

He had not meant to scare her. "Not really stalkers but girls get a crush on me. Luckily, they are in the minority, and overall my fans are happy with the time I give to them off stage. I always take time for signing autographs and taking selfies." He waved a hand to encompass the house. "Having all this might look wonderful, but in truth, I'm a prisoner of fame." He sighed. "This is what living with me will be like, and this is what our kids will endure. The paparazzi won't leave us alone not unless I retire and even then, maybe not."

"The man at the shelter, Gary, said you were as famous as Elvis." She lifted her chin. "I think you need me, Branch, to keep you normal."

Relieved, he let out a long sigh and pulled her into his arms. "Darlin', I've been telling you that for days."

After lunch, Branch followed her into the bedroom. "I'll stay with you and make sure you rest."

"I'm hot." Susie kicked off her boots then shimmied out of her jeans. "I think I'm starting to enjoy sleeping naked." She gave him a slow sexy smile and slowly removed her shirt. "It's your fault. I end up that way in bed every night." Her bra and panties hit the floor.

Branch's mouth went dry. "You are so beautiful. If I had my way, you wouldn't ever wear a stitch of clothing."

"Ha! I bet you won't think the same in another few weeks." She rubbed her belly. "It will be like sleeping with a whale."

He stripped tossing his clothes to the floor then dragged her onto the bed. "Seeing you swelling with my babies makes me happy, and you are the sexiest woman I have ever met." He rolled her onto her back and gazed down at her. "You asked me about songs but since we met my head is filled with *you*. I love the way you make me laugh, and I crave the taste of you, the brush of your lips, and feeling you climax around my cock." He licked a path across her bottom lip then bent to take one succulent nipple in his mouth.

"I love it when you do that." She arched pressing her full breasts into his face demanding more of him. "I want you inside me."

He lifted his head and blew on the wet, erect bud. "Soon, darlin', but the other one will get sad if I don't treat it right."

As he suckled and teased her heavy pink-tipped breasts, she writhed beneath him gripping handfuls of his hair. He wanted to take his time and love her. He kissed down her chest and belly then lifted his gaze to her face. "Show me your pretty silken pussy, darlin'. Open your thighs for me."

"Branch, you drive me to insanity."

"I know." He grinned at her then slipped his tongue between her slick folds.

"I can't take too much more, Branch." She bucked her hips. "I'm dying of pleasure."

"I haven't started loving you yet, darlin'." Holding her hips, he feasted lapping her sweetness and using lips and tongue to rush her to climax. She was so wet, so damn delicious and he had become addicted to her scent. Nothing mattered but pleasing his woman, and he used every skill he had learned. He slid his fingers deep inside her slick pussy, and circled her hard, little nub with his tongue until she panted and moaned. When she trembled against his mouth and cried out, he closed his lips around her clit and suckled extending her orgasm.

Panting with lust, Susie dropped her hands from Branch's thick hair worried she might have hurt the injury to his head, but since the doctor left, he had not mentioned the stitches once. As he tormented her, she let out a feral moan and gave into the pleasure. Flames of delight licked her clit and spread along inflamed nerve endings. Oh boy, he certainly knew how to please a woman. When he kissed his way up her chest, tasting her flesh before grazing her nipples, she trembled in delight. His urgent arousal pressed against her thigh and she wanted him. "*Please,* Branch, I need you."

"You have me." He entered her in one long hard slide then looked into her eyes with such intensity she caught her breath. His eyes reflected her passion, but something had changed, he wet his lips as if to gather courage. "I *love* you, Susie." He examined her gaze from beneath hooded eyelids. "I wanted to tell you now before any results came back. I don't ever want you to believe the twins have any influence on how I feel about you. You are so precious to me, darlin', and if you leave me, I'll mourn your leaving for the rest of my life."

Unable to think, she gaped up at him. He moved inside her, thick and hot making her mindless with erotic delight. She swallowed hard and cupped his handsome face. "I love you too, Branch, and I will forever." Wrapping her legs around his waist, she pulled him down to her. "Kiss me."

His mouth closed over her lips with a hunger she had not experienced from him in all the times they had been together. He was like a thirsty man lapping at a well, his moans of appreciation made her pussy weep around his thick length. When he lifted, his lust for her filled his expression.

"Love makes sex different, like flying through a world of emotional sensations." Branch's mouth lifted in a smile, and he rocked his hips. "Hang on for the ride, darlin'."

With each deep stroke tantalizing flames of deliciousness curled inside her, he made her feel this way each time they made love, but this time, he slowed his pace into a tormenting drawn out ride of erotic euphoria. She clung to him, gripping his broad shoulders and rolling her hips to meet each thrust. Wanting more, faster, deeper, she dug her fingers into his muscular shoulders. "It's too good, Branch, I'm on fire . . . *please* make me come."

"It can't ever be *too* good, darlin'." He grinned down at her. "Suffer a little more, babe. I like to hear that sweet noise you make when you come for me." He swirled his hips and drove in deeper. "Do you like that?"

Breathless, she clung to him riding waves of sexual excitement, so intense her legs trembled, and her stomach tightened as nerve endings screamed for release. He plunged deeper, using his exquisite body to spread her, forcing her higher, building, and building incredible sensations. Knowing he loved her pushed her to a different level of awareness, and when a long moan escaped his lips, she crashed over the edge with him muscles trembling in a sublime joining of erotic bliss. Mindless, she looked into his sweat-soaked face and sighed. "I love you, Branch."

CHAPTER EIGHTEEN

After three days of domestic bliss with the man she loved, Susie checked her phone every few minutes for the doctor to call with the results of the paternity test. Not that she needed to worry, Branch *was* the father, but she wanted the proof, to wave in front of Hunter's nose. Although, both he and Kade had not stepped one foot inside the house since the police left. Branch's calm demeanor and constant attention not to mention glorious sex gave her hope for a perfect future together. After sitting for hours listening to him create songs, she looked forward to taking a break when the front gate bell sounded.

"Why can't people leave us in peace?" Branch rolled his eyes skyward and strolled over to look at the screen. "Dirk, what do you want?"

Dirk's irritated and disjointed voice came through the speaker.

"Why the hell did you turn off your damn phone? The recording studio has been on my back for two days. They need you down there pronto, and in case it slipped your mind you have a photo shoot today at three."

"I told you I wanted some time alone with Susie. Why didn't you make another time, and what's up with the recording studio? I finished cutting the new tracks weeks ago."

"Are you going to let me in and I'll explain?"

"Sure." Branch depressed a button and turned to face her his face glum. "Are you ready to face being out with me in public, darlin'?"

Susie moved to his side and slipped both arms around his neck. "Yes, of course. I'd love to see your music world, and it won't be the first time we've been out in public together."

"This will be different, and I don't want anything to spoil things between us." He nuzzled her neck. "But I guess it will allow you to determine if being my wife is something you could handle."

Branch wants to marry me? Unsure if she should take him seriously or not, she leaned back in his arms and looked into his eyes. "You mean if I pass this test you'll keep me?"

"Oh, you've passed all the tests, darlin', but I want *you* to be sure. I need forever." Branch walked her backward to the sofa and sat her down. He made a big production of walking up and down then cleared his throat and went down on one knee. "I would be honored if you'd be my wife but, and there is a 'but' — I don't want your answer until you've seen the other side of me. I'm Jekyll and Hyde, and you'll need to be able to cope with the 'other' me. The one women want to drag from the stage and strip naked. The player persona is what they expect and trust me, darlin', I play it to the hilt. I'll be that Branch Durham when I'm in public — an asshole. I need you to understand I'm still the same man you love inside the image, and why on stage it's called an 'act' for good reason."

With her heart beating so fast she thought it might burst through her ribs and run away, she stared at him in disbelief. His words percolated slowly through her befuddled brain. He. Had. Asked. Her. To. Marry. Him, and all she could do was gape at him like a nitwit. She sucked in a deep breath and tried to force her trembling lips into a smile then decided to take a different approach. Blubbering about her undying love for him and screaming, "Yes, yes, yes," would not work with a man like Branch Durham. "Hmm, that was a beautiful proposal but have you thought this through at all?"

"I — not really." Branch frowned. "But I meant every word. I want to marry you and as soon as possible. If you'll have me." He looked confused. "Did I miss out anything?"

Worried he might have rushed into a decision because of the twins she smiled sweetly and offered him the chance to back out.

"You're on your knees — that's good but as a man who writes lyrics to make girls cry, the bit after 'I'd be honored if you'd be my wife' was a little strange, don't you think? If you believe my love is unconditional then why include a proviso?" She giggled glad to see his face break into a wide smile.

"Yeah, it was pretty lame, and I don't doubt you love me but this *is* my first proposal." Branch chuckled and rubbed his chin. "You are something else, darlin', and I love every sassy bit of you." He met her gaze. "Is there anything else I need to know before I fall over my tongue again?"

"Hmm, let me see. You didn't have a ring to tempt me into the world of indulgence." She patted him on the arm then cupped his face and gazed into his eyes. "But and here is my proviso — I don't *need* a ring. I would have you penniless and in rags. I love *you*, nothing else matters, not the fame or the money. All I want is *you*, and if you need to be sure, I'll take the fame test, but it won't make any difference."

"Then you'll marry me?" Branch flashed a white grin and pulled her into his arms. "Darlin', you won't be disappointed. I promise to make you happy."

Susie hugged him and rested her chin on his broad shoulder. "Yes, I'll marry you, and whatever life throws at us along the way, we'll face it together."

Her phone rang, and she edged away from him and glanced at the caller ID. "It's the doctor."

"Good, I've been dying to tell the family our secret." Branch pulled her into his arms and placed one large hand protectively over her belly. "Although all this testing is unnecessary they're boys — *my* boys."

Susie raised a brow then grinned at him. "I'll put her on speaker, and we'll find out if you're correct. Hello, this is Susie, Branch is right here, and you're on speaker."

"Congratulations, Mr. Durham, you are the biological father of identical twin boys."

"Hallelujah!" Branch punched the air. "Thank you!"

"I had nothing to do with the results. You did this all by yourselves." Dr. Wright chuckled. *"I'll forward details of the birthing classes I'd like you to attend. I assume you'll want to be with Susie when she gives birth?"*

"I sure do, I wouldn't miss it for the world." Branch's smile lit up the room.

"Good, I'll see you in one month."

The line went dead, and Susie turned to Branch. "I guess we'd better tell your grandma now? I hope she won't be too angry with me."

"With Grandma Durham, you have to ease into telling her things. It's like the story about the man who had to look after his mother's cat when she went away on holiday. Problem was when he went to his mother's house to feed the cat he found it had died from old age."

Susie frowned wondering what this had to do with telling his grandma about her pregnancy. "That's dreadful, what did he do?"

"He didn't want to spoil his mother's holiday, so he told her the cat was on the roof." Branch grinned. "Then he had a few days of stories about trying to get the cat down before he told her the poor thing had died. He sort of eased her into it without giving her a shock."

Leaning back in the chair, Susie stared at him, not quite understanding his logic. "If you tell your grandma I've climbed on the roof, I'm leaving."

"You don't get it, do you, darlin'?" Branch reached for her and pulled her close. "First we tell her we're engaged and plan a quickie wedding. If you don't want all the bells and whistles, it will be a private affair and as quick as possible. I'll ask Dirk to make all the arrangements if you agree. Maybe Vegas is looking good, we could be married and home in a few hours."

She chuckled. "As long as it's not an Elvis impersonator and it's legal. Sure you don't want me to sign a prenuptial?"

"Not a chance, darlin'." He nuzzled her ear. "We'll wait a couple of weeks then tell the family you're pregnant, then about the twins. We'll ease everyone into the news."

"What news?" Dirk strolled into the music room and looked from one to the other.

Susie shrugged as nonchalantly as possible but could not stop grinning. "The cat's on the roof."

* * * *

Later that day the hours spent in the recording studio gave Susie a good insight into how hard Branch worked. Sitting in the control room, he impressed her with his professionalism. After one particularly difficult song, he rewrote the music on the spot and continued until he was satisfied. Not one time, did he lose his cool or become angry with any of the band, and she had wanted to throttle the bass guitarist with her bare hands after he messed up six times in one take. Each time, she listened to Branch's deep beautiful voice her skin pebbled. By the end of the session, he emerged exhausted, but his smile was only for her. She slid off the seat and went to him. "Finished?"

"Yeah, and I'm starving." He glanced at his watch and pulled a face then turned to Dirk. "Call the photographer and let her know we'll be late. I'll need time to shower and eat. Susie hasn't eaten since breakfast, and it's past two."

"Okay." Dirk pulled out his phone. "Before I speak to them, people are going to be asking questions about Susie. What do you want me to say?"

Susie placed a hand on Branch's arm. "Do you think, saying I'm your PA would work? It might give us a little more privacy."

"Good idea." Branch rubbed a towel over his face and turned to Dirk. "I'll use the shower here. Get a table at Julianna's for lunch, somewhere private away from the damn windows."

"Sure." Dirk opened the door to the booth and strode along the passageway.

"Wait here." Branch brushed a soft kiss on her cheek. "I won't be long."

He marched away, bag in hand before she had the chance to tell him she needed to use the bathroom. She waited what seemed like an eternity until the producer got up from his seat, and stretched before going to speak to him. "Can you point me in the direction of the ladies' bathroom?"

"Down the hall past the other studios, turn right, and the bathrooms are on the left." He glanced at her then turned back to the control panel and ignored her.

She ventured out into the hallway following his directions. As she reached the corner, she could hear a woman giggling and Branch's low sexy voice. Not wanting him to believe she had decided to check up on him, she paused in the hallway and leaned against the wall. The other studios had red lights glowing outside, so obviously had other artists recording songs and this might be one of his colleagues. Her bladder at bursting point, she turned the corner and stopped dead. A tall black-haired beauty had one hand gripping the towel around Branch's nude body, the other rested high on his thigh. The way he looked at her with his sexy bedroom eyes made her stomach drop to the floor. His words stabbed into her heart.

"Honey, if I had time, you *know* I'd have you up against the wall fucking you 'till you scream, but I have an appointment, and I'm late." He brushed a kiss over the woman's cheek. "Maybe next time?" He glanced up, and their eyes met. Rather than step away, he acted as if practically making a date with someone else was normal. His brilliant smile did nothing to quell the hurt at seeing him with another woman. "Ah, there you go, my PA is already chasing me."

Catching sight of the ladies' bathroom door, Susie ignored him and slipped inside. She could not face Branch right now or listen to his excuses and wondered what she should do. Could this be the other side of him, she had to cope with if they married? Would she be able to stand seeing a host of women draped all over him? After using the facilities, she called a cab, waited the ten minutes they had advised and headed for the front door. She needed time to think, time away from Branch's sexy gaze and persuasive mouth. The moment she stepped outside, a group of people surged forward, microphones appeared out of nowhere, and men with cameras resting on their shoulders aimed the lenses at her.

"How long have you been involved with Branch Durham? Are you his mermaid?" One red-haired reporter with her eyes flashing looked her up and down.

Susie moved back toward the door, but a huge man barred her way. She drew a deep breath. If they kept on pushing against her, she would topple over. "I'm his PA, that's all. Now if you'll excuse me I have to catch a cab."

"It's okay, Dirk is bringing the car around." Branch moved to her side. "Now why don't you folks leave the girl alone and point those microphones my way? I've just completed my new album, titled, 'The Girl I Left Behind', and I'm late for a photo shoot. Let me through, and I'll take more time with you all later." He pushed her toward Dirk's car.

She climbed inside gripping her purse to her chest and gasping for breath. When Branch pushed a bottle of cold water in her hand, she chanced a glance at him.

"Susie, Susie, Susie." Branch shook his head slowly and met her gaze. "I can read your thoughts, darlin', and you have already let your heart rule your head. I already explained, the image isn't me, remember? Since we first met, it's only been *you*, darlin', and what you witnessed in the hallway is an act. I'm a bad boy, the fans like it that way, and I have women offering me their bodies all the time, it's part of the job." He cupped her face and looked into her eyes. "I would cut out my heart before I hurt you, and I'm faithful, have been even when we were apart. I don't *want* anyone else but you." He let out a long sigh. "This is why I wanted you to wait before you gave me your answer. The women are part of the fame, you have to trust me not to stray, darlin', and why would I when I have everything I need right here?"

She swallowed the lump in her throat. "I failed the first test. When I saw her all over you, I was so jealous, it made me feel sick, and I wanted to run away. I can't turn off the jealousy, Branch. I'm sorry."

"Don't be sorry." Branch pressed warm kisses to the corners of her mouth. "It means you love me, and I promise to try my best to avoid making you jealous, but shit happens, like before. Do you know, Andrea came right into the men's bathroom and accosted me? She is the lead singer of the Dovetails, and with the press outside the building she'll probably tell them we're going together." He grinned. "She'll look a bit stupid when I marry you, huh?"

"*You* are getting married?" Dirk stopped at the lights and turned to stare at Branch.

"Yeah, as soon as you can arrange it in Vegas. We want it kept private if possible." Branch pulled her under one arm. "Something else but I have to swear you to secrecy."

"Sure, you know I can be trusted." Dirk moved the car through the lights.

"Susie is having twins, boys." Branch gazed into her eyes and emotion filled his expression. "My boys. I don't want anyone to know until I tell the family."

"Congratulations." Dirk pulled into the parking lot of a restaurant. "I'll make the wedding arrangements as soon as I get back to the office." He cleared his throat. "Ah . . . perhaps you'd better explain about the photographer before we arrive?"

Susie moved her attention to Branch, who pulled a face then shrugged. She wet her lips. "If there's a problem it would be better if I took a cab back to the ranch."

"It's no big deal." Branch chewed on his bottom lip as if making a decision and then took both her hands. "The photographer's name is Zoe, and we dated before I met you. I didn't love her and when she wanted to bring her girlfriend into our bed—"

Susie pulled her hands away. "Stop! I don't want to know the gory details." She reached for the water bottle and drained it then leveled her gaze at him. "Just tell me when we meet women if you've dated them, so I don't look like some naïve idiot even if I am, okay?"

"Sure. No secrets, I promise." Branch glanced at Dirk. "If we want her to pass as my PA give her your iPad to carry into the restaurant."

"Good idea." Dirk handed it over and chuckled. "Maybe walk beside me, then everyone will think you're with me."

"You wish." Branch slid from the car and opened the door for her. "Susie stays with me."

Susie walked beside him and with his hand firmly on her back, headed inside the restaurant. When all eyes turned toward them, watching every step toward the table, she held her breath. *Oh boy, this will be my life from now on, and I have yet to tell Grandma Durham, I'm pregnant.*

CHAPTER NINETEEN

Two days later in a small wedding chapel in Las Vegas, Susie stood beside her handsome cowboy and stumbled through the vows she had written to bind her to Branch. His beautiful heart-stopping, gorgeous words made her cry. By the time they exchanged rings, tears dripped off her chin. She accepted the tissue Dirk pushed into her hand and caught Kade's uncomfortable expression. Dabbing at her face, she looked up at Branch, who gazed down at her with his trademark brilliant smile, but this time it was only for her.

"Darlin', if you keep crying, this nice man will think this is a shotgun wedding, and Kade looks fit to kill me right now." Branch pulled her into his arms surrounding her with his unique scent. "Dear Lord, you're trembling." He brushed a kiss over her lips and rubbed her back. "Talk to me."

In his arms, a warm safeness surrounded her. She turned her head and blew her nose. "You said such beautiful things, and my vows were so feeble."

"I don't think promising to love me forever was lame. I went a little misty too." Branch kissed her possessively then sucked her bottom lip inside his hot mouth and moaned. "I *love* you, Susie Durham. Don't that sound fine?"

"Yes." Susie wet her lips tasting him on her tongue. "I love you too."

"Why don't you allow my wife to fix your makeup then we can take the photographs?" The marriage celebrant smiled benevolently at her and waved his wife forward. "We don't have to rush, Mr. Durham was kind enough to book the chapel for the entire afternoon."

"Thank you." Susie smoothed down the skirt to the sleeveless white silk dress she had purchased earlier and handed

Dirk her flowers then squeezed Branch's arm. "Do you mind? I'll only be five minutes."

"We have forever, darlin'. Take all the time you need."

She followed the woman into a bride's parlor adjacent to the chapel and took a seat in front of a white dressing table complete with large vases of plastic flowers. "I feel such an idiot."

"It happens to a lot of young women, and you've married a celebrity, no wonder you are overcome with nerves." The woman poured a glass of water over ice and handed it to her. "You look fine. My husband thought you needed a few minutes to gather yourself. My, my, seeing Branch Durham in the flesh, made my heart skip a beat, and you are the lucky girl to have married him."

"Yes, I am." Susie sipped the water then tidied her hair. She had used a tiny amount of makeup, preferring her natural look, and apart from wet eyelashes, she looked fine. "I'm ready to go."

She strolled into the chapel and took in Branch's handsome face. Oh boy, he was one delicious man dressed in a suit, but she preferred him in his skin-tight jeans and sexy muscle-hugging tee shirts. When he held out his hand to her, she went to him. "I'm okay now, no more tears."

"You are so beautiful." Branch kissed her tenderly then bent to whisper close to her ear. "I can't wait to kiss you all over." He nuzzled her neck. "Maybe you can ride *me* tonight?"

Her face grew hot at Dirk's bark of laughter. *Oh, my God, he heard.* She lifted her chin and kissed the corners of Branch's wicked grin. "Maybe, I will."

After the photographs and document signing, the wedding group rode the elevator to the roof and climbed into the Durham helicopter. She took the headphones Branch gave her and pulled them over her ears. As Kade took the chopper into the air, she gave Branch a playful punch on the arm. "I didn't even get to play the slots."

"Maybe next time." Branch grinned at her. "I didn't want anyone seeing us and have the paparazzi crashing our wedding.

This is our day, and I didn't want it spoiled by a media frenzy." He tapped Dirk on the shoulder. "You did remember to get the memory card from the camera, didn't you?"

"Oh, yeah." Dirk held a small chip between thumb and finger. "It cost you two hundred bucks."

"Cheap at the price." Branch chuckled and took Susie's hand. "Are you ready to face my grandma?"

"I guess." She stared at her gold wedding band. "I hope she won't be angry we didn't invite the family to the wedding."

"I don't think so, she understands the restrictions of my profession, and she won't ride in a chopper. Kade was here to represent the family." He cleared his throat. "Hunter and Lance might be a little miffed, but I doubt it. They'll understand the need for secrecy."

Susie leaned against her new delicious husband and sighed. "Who do you think will be the next Durham boy to marry?"

"Not me." Kade's voice came through her headphones. "I'm not seeing anyone, and Hunter, well he'll never find a woman to melt his cold heart."

"Why? What happened to him?"

"His high school sweetheart cheated on him." Kade cleared his throat. "He is very competitive, and I guess, he figured he'd lost that fight. He dates but never gets close anymore. Me, I've yet to find a woman who will put up with me." He chuckled deep and low. "I like to stay out late, I get into brawls, and women usually run for the hills. I'm better staying single."

"Oh shit." Dirk leaned forward and stared out the window. "We just went over your ranch, and there are TV vehicles everywhere." He flicked a glance over his shoulder. "They know."

"I'll take you to see grandma, and when you're ready to go home, I can put the chopper down at the back of your house. No one will be able to bother you." Kade glanced at Dirk. "Maybe you need to call the cops to have them disbursed."

"Nah." Branch peered out the window. "If they don't see me, they'll go soon enough, and trust me, we aren't planning on going outside for some time." He turned and winked at her. "Are we, darlin'?"

A few moments later, she took Branch's hand and walked into the sitting room of the Durham Ranch, to find Hunter and Grandma Durham in deep conversation. Both people stopped talking and looked up at the same time. Heat filled Susie's cheeks, and she clung to Branch's hand as if it were a life preserver.

"I guess congratulations are in order?" Hunter stood and offered Branch his hand. "You should have told me. I could have arranged a prenuptial agreement for you." He smiled at her. "Welcome to the family."

Hunter's eagle eyes bored into her. He obviously had little trust in women. She swallowed the need to run away and smiled back. "Thank you."

"There is no prenupt." Branch shook Hunter's hand then turned to his grandmother. "Are you happy I'm finally married?"

"Yes, I'm happy." Grandma Durham peered at Susie then nodded as if confirming a suspicion. "When are you due, dear?"

* * * *

Safe in his own home, Branch pulled his bride into the bedroom then burst out laughing. "Oh my God, she knew all the time." He flopped down on the bed pulling Susie with him. "Kade told me once, she could tell when a horse was in foal months before it showed. It looks like she has the talent for people as well. I'll give her a few weeks before we tell her about the twins and then trust me, she'll be insisting on holding a baby shower for you."

"I loved the expression on Hunter's face when you told him about not having a prenupt. He almost blew a cog." Susie wiped the tears of laughter from her pink cheeks. "Apart from that, I think it went quite well."

"Ah-huh, there is one more thing, I need to do." He ran his hand up her smooth bare thigh and hooked his fingers into the elastic of her panties. "I want to see my wife naked." He tugged, and the wispy thin fabric disintegrated.

He loved the breathy moan that escaped Susie's lips the moment he spread her pussy and circled her clit. "Do you want me, darlin', because I'm hungry for some loving?"

"God, yes." She fumbled at the buttons of his shirt. "I need to touch you."

He flipped her over, unzipped her dress and had her naked in seconds. His clothes followed, and he lay back on the pillows. "Come here, straddle me. I want to see your breasts and tight nipples dangling in front of my face."

"That sounds like fun, but now you are all mine, I need something too." She bent and licked a tormenting path up the inside of his thigh. "You taste so good, but I want to try more."

When she suckled his sac with tender care, Branch gasped and forced his muscles to relax. Her warm, wet mouth moved to his length, and he moaned and lifted his hips. "Taste all you want, darlin', but if you stay too long, my plan to see you riding me will be over real soon."

When she swallowed him, he groaned and reached for her. "Oh, God, that is so good, but I want to be inside you."

"Okay." Susie straddled his thighs. "I love the way you feel in my mouth."

He lifted her over his throbbing erection and pulled her down to kiss her cherry lips. When she lifted her head and gazed down at him, her eyes slightly unfocused with passion, he bent to capture an erect nipple in his mouth. He watched her face as he lavished attention on one bud and then the other. Against his belly, her juices flowed hot and wet. "I want you to ride me, lean forward and I'll slip inside your pretty pussy."

She complied dangling her beautiful breasts in his face and he sunk into paradise. "Sit up, oh yeah, just like that." He rolled his hips. "Move with me, darlin', how does that feel?"

"Oh, Branch, you feel so much bigger this way." She leaned back pushing her full breasts toward him. "Oh yes, harder, push in harder."

He drove into her, watching her breasts bound with each thrust. She looked so beautiful, her face flushed and her pussy open for his gaze. He stroked her clit, and she went wild and bounced on him, pushing his control to the limit. Under his fingers, the hard bead throbbed, and she stiffened before her slick passage gripped him, massaging him into erotic oblivion. Shuddering he joined her in a mind-blowing climax.

He held her twitching body against him, rocking his still hard erection inside her to extend her orgasm. "I *love* you, Mrs. Durham."

"I'll love you *forever*." She pressed warm kisses to his chest.

He chuckled and nuzzled her ear. "Darlin', forever won't be long enough."

THE END

AUTHOR BIOGRAPHY

H.C. Brown is a multi-published, multi-genre, bestselling, award-winning author.

In 2016, she was delighted to be named Luminosity Publishing's Bestselling Author of 2015.

In 2015, she was delighted to be named Luminosity Publishing's Bestselling Author of 2014.

In 2015, *Highlander in the Mist* was placed 3rd in Historical, and *Rock 'n' Leather* was placed 3rd GLBT in the Easychair Bookshop Competition.

In 2015, *Highlander in The Mist* was nominated in The Romance Reviews 2015 Readers' Awards.

In 2011, she was delighted to receive nominations in three categories in the 2011 CAPA Awards: Favorite Author, Best GLBT Romance, and Best Science Fiction Romance.

She was nominated for Best Historical M/M in the 2013, Goodreads Book of Year Awards.

H.C writes about strong alpha male heroes and girl next door heroines in complex settings, and all her stories have happy endings.

H.C. welcomes feedback from her readers.

Connect with H.C.

http://www.hcbrown-author.com/

H.C. BROWN

LUMINOSITY
PUBLISHING